M000032916

Emergency Case

RICHARD L. MABRY, MD

AUTHOR'S NOTES

Books are not written in a vacuum. That's not true of most novels, and it certainly isn't with this one. I could list dozens of folks who have helped me on this road to writing, but below is the short list.

Without the support of my agent, Rachelle Gardner of Books & Such Literary Agency, I would never have reached this point in my writing journey. Thanks, Rachelle, for believing in me.

My first reader is also my biggest supporter (and sometimes my severest critic). Thanks to Kay Mabry, my wife, for keeping me focused. When you say, "This isn't up to your standards," I've learned to believe you and make a change. I've never regretted it.

As is the case with all my indie-published work, my thanks go to Dineen Miller for designing and executing a great cover, to Barbara Scott for applying her editorial genius, and to Virginia Smith for getting this book into print. And, of course, I'm grateful to you, my loyal reader, for reading this book and helping spread the word about it and the other novels I've been fortunate enough to see published.

Over a decade ago, when I set out to write a book about my struggles after the death of my first wife, a book that was published as *The Tender* Scar, I had no idea that God would lead me along this path of writing. I'm amazed and a bit awe-struck by all that has happened. But, as always, *Soli Deo Gloria*—to God be the glory.

Richard L. Mabry, MD

Books by Richard L. Mabry, MD

Novels of Medical Suspense
Code Blue
Medical Error
Diagnosis Death
Lethal Remedy
Stress Test
Heart Failure
Critical Condition
Fatal Trauma
Miracle Drug
Medical Judgment
Cardiac Event
Guarded Prognosis

Novellas
Rx Murder
Silent Night, Deadly Night
Doctor's Dilemma
Surgeon's Choice
Emergency Case

Non-Fiction
The Tender Scar: Life After the Death of A Spouse

Copyright 2018, Richard L. Mabry

1

Jack Harbaugh sat at his mahogany desk scribbling notes on a yellow pad, several law books open beside him. This was a particularly ticklish tax case, and he'd promised his CPA friend to have an interpretation soon. He was at a critical point when his secretary's voice over the intercom interrupted him.

"Mr. Alba is here."

Mr. Alba? Then Jack remembered. This was the case he didn't want to take. But he'd allowed himself to be pressured.

Jack redid the top button of his dress shirt and cinched his tie. "Send him in."

The man who entered his office was, at first glance, the type of individual that Jack and his partners cultivated as clients. His dark hair appeared freshly cut and styled, his clean-shaven jaw bore not a trace of five o'clock shadow, his suit draped perfectly to conceal a stocky frame, and his white shirt gleamed.

But then Jack looked into Alba's eyes, and they told him all he needed to know. He had seen eyes like that only once before—in a criminal who was amoral to the point of having no concern for others or even for his own life.

Jack stood but didn't extend his hand. Instead, he gestured toward one of the two client chairs across from his desk. Alba didn't seem upset by Jack's failure to shake hands. He nodded, seated himself, crossed his legs, and looked directly at the attorney. "What do you want to know about the case?"

"First, let's get some things settled." Jack resumed his chair and opened the center drawer of his desk. He pulled out a contract of representation and shoved it toward Alba. "Read this. If you want me to represent you, sign it."

Alba scribbled his signature without reading the document. Then he pulled a fat envelope from his shirt pocket and put it atop the contract. "Here's the fee ... in cash, just as you were promised." He held up his hand. "And I won't need a receipt."

"Whether you want one or not, I'm going to note that I've been paid, and report this as income." Jack put the envelope, still unopened, into his top drawer along with the signed contract. "Now tell me about the traffic stop and the ticket that came afterward."

The story was pretty much what Jack had already heard. Alba was pulled over because he fit the description of a man the police were looking for. There was no other reason for the stop, although that point was arguable. What was clear to Jack, however, was there was no legal justification for the search of Alba's car, a search that turned up a small amount of marijuana in the glove compartment.

When Jack had enough details, he nodded. "We should be able to get you off. Maybe a fine, but I doubt even that." His mind went back to what he'd been told previously.

Supposedly, this was a "slam-dunk." He wondered if that was because the fix was already in with the judge. Whether it was or not, he'd do his best. That was what he was being paid handsomely for.

"You really need to get this case dismissed," Alba said.

"I'm pretty sure we can do that," Jack responded. "Trust me."

"I mean, I can't have the law nosing around after me. I'm due to complete a gun buy a few days after my court date. What if some eager DA starts looking too closely at me?"

"I'm not certain what you mean, but maybe you shouldn't tell me anymore."

But Alba kept talking. He told Jack he was a key figure in an illegal transfer of weapons that was to take place in the early morning hours behind a local gun store in about a week. The clandestine event would involve pistols, long guns, and ammunition, all of which would bring at least a hundred thousand dollars when it was resold. Probably more, Alba said.

Jack held up both hands, palm outward. "Stop! I can't hear this."

Alba was genuinely puzzled. "Why not? You're my attorney, aren't you? Isn't all this privileged information?"

"No. It's true that I'm your attorney, but I'm also an officer of the court. If you tell me about a crime that's going to be committed, I'm obliged to report it. Privilege doesn't cover that."

"Well, whether that contract I signed protects me or not, you certainly can't report this to the authorities. If anything happens to stop this deal, my boss will see to it that the person who leaked the information never talks again."

He looked at Jack with those dead eyes. "That means either you or me ... or both."

Dr. Kelly Harbaugh had just sat down at her desk and picked up a few papers when the senior partner of her group, Dr. Cathy Sewell, tapped on the doorframe. "Got a second?"

"Sure." Kelly gestured toward the chair across the desk from her. "I was going to talk with you as soon as you had a break."

Cathy looked directly at her friend and colleague. "Is everything okay?"

Kelly knew what Cathy meant. She took a deep breath. "You mean the way I've been acting?"

Cathy nodded.

"Jack and I have always had a good marriage, but recently he's seemed a bit distant. I guess that's normal, especially between a doctor and an attorney." Kelly fixed pleading eyes on her colleague. "You and Will went through that, didn't you?"

"Did we have problems?" Cathy smiled. "Sure, but it didn't have anything to do with our professions. Despite what you may read or hear, no marriage is a constant rendition of "Hearts and Flowers." Will and I have our differences just like any other couple. Since he was practicing law, there were times he was so preoccupied with a case that he seemed to pay no attention to me at all. And I understood. I'm sure there were times when the shoe was on the other foot. But it was temporary, and it was soon over." She leaned forward. "Is that what's going on with you and Jack right now?"

Kelly nodded. "The past week or more he's been so ... preoccupied. Sometimes it's as though his mind is somewhere else. We used to talk about everything, but now it's like he's pulled into his shell. I can't help thinking—"

"Wondering if it's something you did?"

"Yes."

Cathy shook her head. "It's more likely something at work bothering him."

"I guess you're right," Kelly said. "Maybe it's a case, but his little firm mainly handles wills, real-estate transactions, stuff like that. I don't think he's seen the inside of a courtroom more than half a dozen times since law school."

"Do you tell each other about everything in your practice?" Cathy said. "Will and I don't. I mean, if there's something big I try to share it with him, and vice-versa. But sometimes things slip through. Maybe he's worried about an issue he hasn't told you about."

"I hope that's it."

"I know you and Jack have only been married a short time, but these things iron themselves out. You'll see."

Kelly watched Cathy leave. Why didn't she feel reassured?

Jack Harbaugh stared at the eggs on his plate. Kelly had asked him her usual question about what he wanted for breakfast, and although he wasn't really hungry, he'd decided it was easier to ask her to scramble a couple of eggs than get into a long discussion. That would come soon enough.

"Is something wrong with your breakfast?"

"No, this is fine." He picked up his fork and moved the eggs around, but before he could start eating he saw Kelly bow her head. She was going to ask a blessing, whether he joined in or not. He paused, eyes down but open, until she finished. He realized that over the past several days he'd been so engrossed in Alba's case that he'd even neglected their habit of praying before meals. But soon he could tell her what was going on.

She raised her head and looked at him. "Jack, is something bothering you?"

"I'm preoccupied with a case. I can't talk about it yet. I promise in a day or two I'll have things wound up." *One way or another.*

"I didn't know you had many cases that went to trial. Is this one coming up soon?"

Jack shook his head. He didn't want to talk about it— not yet. "Actually, I appeared before a judge a couple of days ago. The case was dismissed."

"So, what's still going on?"

"I ... I still have one thing to do."

He moved his eggs around on his plate again. Suddenly, the sight of them was more than Jack could stomach. He used his uneaten toast to cover the almost untouched food. Then he pushed back from the table. "I've got to go."

Without a word, Kelly also rose from the table. She discarded the remains of her breakfast into the sink and put her dishes in the dishwasher. Then she picked up her husband's plate. She scraped his uneaten eggs into the garbage disposal but didn't comment on his odd behavior.

Jack stopped at the doorway from the kitchen into the attached garage, briefcase in hand. "I'll see you tonight." He paused before adding, "I love you."

Kelly didn't even look up from the sink.

Usually, they parted with a kiss and a mutual exchange of "I love you." Today, his "I love you" sounded perfunctory, even to his ears, but it was all he could manage. His mind was already on the conversation he planned to have with his partner. Then, he'd go to the police and tell them the rest of what he knew. But first he had to tell Ainsley.

Kelly stepped into the garage almost on Jack's heels. The unheated space was cold, so she shrugged deeper into her coat. Of course, it was December, so what else should she expect? Here in this part of Texas, snow in December was unusual, but not unheard of, and it had come overnight—at least a light coating of the white stuff.

Kelly slid into the driver's seat of her car. She glanced to her right at her husband preparing to climb into his BMW. She decided that tonight, no matter what, she'd find out what was bothering him.

She pushed the button to open the garage door, then started her Subaru sedan. Her mind still on her relationship with her husband, Kelly looked briefly in the rearview mirror and saw a dusting of snow on the roof of the house directly across the alley. She spared a moment's thought to how the frozen precipitation might affect the traction of her vehicle and decided she'd have no problem. She slipped her car into reverse and backed down the slightly inclined drive.

Her tires took hold easily, but nevertheless she kept her speed slow. She had done this so many times, she was on automatic pilot. Kelly occasionally glanced at the rearview mirror as she cleared the garage but didn't bother to look at the images the car's back-up camera displayed. Suddenly she felt a bump, and the backward motion of her car hesitated, then stopped. Kelly shook her head. *Please, not this morning. I'm already running late.*

She looked in the car's rearview mirror but couldn't see what had stopped her. Kelly tapped the accelerator, but the obstruction held her car fast. She put the transmission into park and climbed out.

As she made her way carefully to the rear of the car, Kelly hoped that what had impeded her was just a mound of snow. A few moments with the shovel could take care of that. She might even be able to pull forward a bit, then put the car in reverse, push down on the accelerator, power over the obstruction, and be on her way.

But after she rounded the car's rear bumper, she realized in horror the bump she'd felt wasn't snow. It was the body of a man lying in the driveway. His left hand, which lay outstretched beneath the right rear wheel of her still-running car, seemed to be reaching out to her.

Kelly bent over and took the free hand of the corpse to feel for a pulse, but—as she knew before she started—there was none. The body was cold and stiff. There was no need to call for help. The man was beyond that. The next thing was to notify the police. But first she had to tell her husband.

She rose from her position next to the corpse and shouted at Jack, who still sat in his car with the door partially open, waiting for Kelly to clear the driveway. "Jack, come here. There's a dead man in our driveway."

Jack's mind was elsewhere as he walked out of the house and into the garage with his silent wife right behind him. When he felt the cold wind as she opened the garage door, he grumbled and buttoned his topcoat before sliding behind the wheel. His mind was elsewhere as Kelly backed out. When he looked up and saw her car idling halfway down the driveway, he shook his head. *Now what's she done?* He glanced at the time on his cell phone. Whatever it was, he hoped it wouldn't slow him down.

He prepared to start his BMW, but before he fully closed the car door he stopped to listen. His wife was yelling something, but at first, he wasn't certain he'd heard her correctly.

"Jack, come here. There's a dead man in our driveway."

"What?"

She repeated the sentence, a bit louder this time. Jack scrambled out of his car and moved toward the back of Kelly's still-running Subaru. "That's ridiculous," he said. But his heart thumped in his chest, remembering Alba's warning.

"See for yourself," she managed to say and crossed her arms, hugging herself.

In a few more steps, he reached the corpse. He bent over and looked carefully at the man who lay there, and when his gaze reached the face, Jack knew this was going to be a long morning—no, make that a long day.

2

Kelly started to shut off the ignition of her car, which was still running, but then remembered the TV shows she'd watched. She decided she should leave everything as it was until the police arrived. *Don't touch a thing.*

The two policemen who responded to the 9-1-1 call arrived in less than twenty minutes—an eternity in her mind. They handled the situation as though finding a dead body in someone's driveway was routine. Maybe it was for them, but for Kelly it was far from an everyday experience. As she stood back and let the police do their work, she shivered—not just from the cold but from nervousness as well. After they asked a few questions, the more senior of the patrolmen told Kelly she could shut off the ignition of her car. Then they'd wait for the detectives.

"May I make a call to my office?"

The patrolman didn't even look up from writing in his notebook. "Sure. Just don't go near the body."

"I already have. I'm a physician, and I checked to make sure the man was dead." She took a deep breath. "He is."

The patrolman continued writing. "I know." He waved Kelly off.

She moved into the shelter of the garage and used her cell phone to call the office of the three-doctor family practice group where she worked. No one was in yet, so her call was taken by the answering service. The operator promised she'd relay the message as soon as the receptionist checked in. Kelly ended her call and looked at Jack, who was on his phone as well.

In a few minutes, a black Chevrolet pulled up and parked at an angle behind Kelly's Subaru, which still sat in the driveway. The Chevy effectively blocked both the driveway and the alley it fed into, but the car's occupants didn't seem to care. The newly arrived vehicle was unmarked, although it was obvious even to a casual observer that it was a police car. A bottom-of-the-line sedan, a computer on a swing arm visible through the windshield, and strobe lights only partially hidden behind the grill marked it as clearly as if the words were emblazoned on the doors.

Two people, a man and a woman, exited and headed for the corpse and the patrolmen standing next to it. They wore civilian clothes, but both had the unmistakable look of police.

After covering their shoes with paper booties, both bent over and looked at the dead man. One of them—the woman—started to reach over and turn him, but Kelly heard the man say, "Let's wait for the medical examiner and crime scene people. Want to call and see if you can hurry them? I'm freezing."

The woman turned away, pulled out her cell phone, and made a call. At the same time, the man started walking toward Kelly. He was tall and thin, with receding black hair. Despite the cold, he wore neither a hat nor topcoat. His suit was neat, his white shirt clean and well-pressed, and he wore a conservative tie. She wouldn't have taken him for a detective by the way he dressed, but when Kelly got a good look at his face, there was no doubt in her mind. He looked at the world through piercing blue eyes that seemed to see into the soul of the person he focused on.

"I'm Detective Tom Carmody," he said. "The woman with me is my partner, Detective Amy Hancock. Tell me what happened here."

Jack hurried over before Kelly could say a word. "I'm her husband and an attorney. I think I should be present during all phases of questioning here."

Carmody looked at Jack with the contempt he'd give something he'd just scraped off the bottom of his shoe. "Counselor, I'll get to you in a minute. It appears this car is your wife's, and I assume she was driving it." He inclined his head toward the blue Subaru that sat silent, the corpse still trapped beneath its right rear wheel. "I haven't accused her of anything. I'm just getting her story."

"But—"

The detective leaned closer to Jack. "I'm taking a statement, Counselor. When you hear me say something that includes the words, 'You have the right to an attorney,' feel free to stick your nose in. Otherwise, step away and let me get on with finding out what happened here."

Carmody turned back to Kelly. "Now, as you were saying?"

Just then the female detective joined the group. Whereas Carmody's complexion was so pale it appeared he never saw the sun, Detective Hancock's was dark brown bordering on ebony. She was considerably shorter than Carmody, and in contrast with his thin build, she was full-figured. Gray slacks showed beneath her quilted jacket. Short brown hair peeked around the edges of her knit cap. Her brown eyes seemed kinder than Carmody's, but she, like him, had the underlying take-charge attitude that Kelly figured was the mark of all police officers, whether in uniform or plain clothes.

"A crime scene crew is on the way, as well as a deputy medical examiner." She looked at Kelly, who was shivering. "We're going to tie up this area for a while. Why don't we go into your house? It's sort of chilly out here."

In the living room, Jack stood by and kept his mouth closed—with effort—until after Kelly gave her statement. At that point Carmody turned to a fresh page in his notebook and looked at Jack.

"Okay, Counselor, now it's your turn. You've been anxious to get on the record, so this is your chance. Let's start with your name."

Jack had been thinking, and the more he considered his situation, the more he realized he should keep what he knew to himself... at least until he'd talked with his partner. "Jack Harbaugh. I'm an attorney here in town. I came out of the house. I heard my wife say there was a dead man in our driveway. I looked and confirmed it."

"And?"

"That's all I have to say right now."

As Jack was afraid he would, Detective Carmody moved immediately to the question he wasn't yet ready to answer. "Your wife said she had no idea who the dead man was." He scanned his notes. "Her exact words were, 'I've never seen him before.' So how about you, Counselor?"

Here it was already. When given the option, tell the truth. But only to answer the question. Don't volunteer more. "Yes. When I got a bit closer, I recognized the dead man."

"And?" Carmody raised his eyebrows. "Who was he? How did you know him?"

Jack took in a deep breath. "He's a client I represented in court a couple of days ago. His name is Eric Alba."

Carmody's expression didn't change. Hancock turned to a fresh page in her notebook and said, "Spell that name."

Jack did.

"And why would his corpse end up in your driveway?" Carmody asked.

"I have no idea."

The expressions of both Carmody and Hancock said, "We'll see about that." Jack was certain that, before it was all over, he would tell the police the whole story. But first he needed to have a conversation—one he dreaded.

Kelly didn't know why Jack was so hesitant to speak to the police. Then again, she ordinarily didn't ask him about his cases, just as she didn't tell him about most of her patients. But this was different. The dead man in their driveway had apparently been a client of her husband's. She wanted to hear what Jack told the police about ... what was his name? Adams? Anders? No, Alba. Eric Alba. Had she heard that name before? She didn't think so.

"What was the case about?" Carmody asked.

"I think any information on that is privileged," Jack said, hoping the detective didn't know the law.

Carmody shook his head. "Counselor, if you passed your bar exam you know that it's not difficult for the police to find out what a trial is about. Perhaps what the deceased told you is privileged, although I think it's been argued that privilege may die when the client does. We can let the District Attorney haggle with you on that. All I want to know right now is what was the charge you defended Alba against."

Kelly leaned forward to catch her husband's next words. They were spoken quietly, as though Jack didn't want anyone else to hear, but she caught them clearly.

"He was charged with drug possession."

"What drug?"

Jack hesitated. "A small amount of marijuana."

Detective Carmody looked Jack in the eye. "And was he guilty of that?"

"The court agreed with my argument that the traffic stop that led to the discovery of the drug was illegal," Jack replied. "Everything that followed was fruit of the poisoned tree. They dismissed the charge."

The police crime scene specialists had photographed, measured, and in general memorialized everything in the area. Finally, the Medical Examiner came in and spoke softly to Carmody. He nodded and told Kelly she could move her car forward. She noticed Jack followed her out of the house. He was probably anxious to get going. She was too.

In the garage, Kelly got out of her Subaru and joined Jack, who was leaning against the fender of his BMW. The two watched the ME conferring with the detectives. They couldn't hear what was being said, but the ME knelt, rolled the body away from him, and used a pen to point to the back of Alba's head. The detectives looked where he was pointing and nodded.

"What do you suppose they found?" Kelly asked.

"I don't know," Jack replied. "Usually they're interested in cause of death, but that sometimes isn't determined for certain until after an autopsy."

"Can you see what he's pointing at?"

Jack shrugged. "I'm wondering about bullet wounds, but Alba's dark hair is so long and matted I can't tell—at least, not at this distance."

Kelly looked at her watch. "How much longer do you think we'll be here?"

"One thing I've learned in what few dealings I've had with the police—they're never in a hurry."

Kelly looked at the alley, now full of official vehicles. "Yes, and they don't seem to mind blocking a roadway."

It was another half hour, perhaps longer, before the ME climbed into his car and left, followed in short order by the van bearing the body of Eric Alba. The crime scene specialists seemed to have broadened their field of interest, scuffing snow away and even using a metal detector in the area just past Kelly and Jack's driveway. The two detectives were also still present, getting periodic reports from the four uniformed officers who were now at the crime scene.

Finally, Kelly couldn't stand it. "I'm going to ask them how much longer."

Jack shook his head. "I wouldn't try to hurry them. In my limited experience—"

Kelly spoke over her shoulder as she turned and started toward the detectives. "Well, I don't have any experience with bodies in our driveway, but I think they need to let us get on with our lives." She marched over to Detective Carmody. "How much longer are you all going to be?"

He held up a finger as one of the police officers approached. Carmody addressed the patrolman. "Checked them all?"

"Yes, sir. We've gone to all the houses that face this alley and viewed the images from the security cameras of the people who were home."

"Any of them capture what we need?"

The police officer started to answer. Then he looked at Kelly and hesitated. "Maybe. I'll forward the images in question to your smart phone, and you can take a look at them."

At that moment, a member of the crime scene team called out, "Detective, I think I've found what we're looking for."

What could that be? Kelly had noticed there had been enough traffic down the alley before all this to obliterate individual tire tracks. The snow might have retained footprints, but would they be pertinent? Other than that, what could the team members have found?

The woman, who was wearing dark blue coveralls, stood over something just down the alley from the driveway where Alba's body was found. Carmody walked toward her, and Kelly fell in behind. *No one has stopped me, and I was the one who ran over the body. If it's about how this man died…*

"Here it is," the tech said, pointing down to where snow had been swept away, revealing a pistol that lay in the grass on the verge of the alley.

"Okay to move it?"

"We already have pictures of this where we found it." The criminologist put a pencil through the trigger guard, lifted the gun, and handed it, pencil and all, to Carmody.

He looked at the pistol, then turned to Kelly. "Do either you or your husband have a gun in the house?"

"Yes. Jack was advised by several of the attorneys in town to carry a pistol, so he got one and a permit early in his practice."

"Does his look like this?"

She inclined her head toward the one the detective held. "I don't know much about guns, but I think Jack's is sort of like that one."

"We can get a search warrant, but there's an easier way. Let's talk with your husband and see if he minds showing us his pistol."

When the two detectives and Kelly approached Jack, he quickly ended his cell phone conversation. "I'll call you back. Maybe the detectives are about to turn me loose." He stowed his phone. "Yes?"

"Counselor, the deceased was apparently killed by a bullet to the back of the head. The ME thinks it was a single shot from a .38 caliber weapon, probably an execution-style killing. I understand you have a pistol. Would you mind showing it to us?"

Jack frowned. "I know what you're up to. You want to see if my gun is the one that killed Alba. Well, that's ridiculous. My pistol is right where I always keep it." He strode toward his car, opened the door, and pulled out a leather briefcase with the initials JH on it. Jack opened the case and said, "See for yourself."

"Get it out for us, please. Just pull the gun out by the barrel," Carmody said. "Keep your finger away from the trigger."

Kelly noticed that both detectives let their hands hover over their hips where holstered weapons were concealed by their jackets. Jack held the briefcase with one hand, and rummaged inside it with his other, moving aside papers and other material. In a moment, a worried look crossed his face. Then he looked at Carmody, the expression on his face equal parts of surprise and anxiety. "It's gone."

Carmody held up the evidence bag that contained the pistol the crime scene tech found. "So, is this your gun?"

"I can't say," Jack replied. "I mean, the one I had was a Ruger six-shot revolver, like that one. But I didn't scratch my initials on it or anything."

"Do we have your permission to search your house to see if yours is somewhere inside?"

Jack thought about that for a few moments, but finally gave permission.

Carmody stopped two officers who were about to climb into their patrol car. "Wait. Get the other two patrolmen who are still here to help you. We have permission to search the premises for a pistol." He explained to them what they were looking for. After almost an hour spent searching, they reported negative findings.

"Let's assume that's my revolver," Jack said. "You can even assume it's the weapon that killed Alba. That still doesn't implicate me. Obviously, someone took it from my briefcase. We don't know who did it, or when that happened."

"Maybe someone stole it during the party we had last week," Kelly said.

"My briefcase was inside the house at that time, so I guess that's possible. But I take it with me to lots of places—my office, court, even other people's offices. Besides that, I don't really know when I last saw the gun." Jack looked at the detective. "I suppose you'll fire comparison bullets from that pistol and see if they match up with the one the pathologist takes out of Alba's head."

"That's the usual routine," Carmody said. "Did you report the pistol as stolen?"

"No. I didn't know it was gone until you had me look for it."

"So, we have only your word."

Jack found that, in spite of the cold, he was sweating. "Am I a suspect?"

"Let's just say you're a person of interest." The detective called over to the criminalist who stood nearby. "I'm sure the Counselor here won't mind submitting to a test for gunshot residue."

They moved once more into the house, where Jack allowed paraffin to be applied to his hands. This test had been updated through the years from the old nitrate test, and now included spectroscopy. Jack hoped modern science wouldn't fail him.

"And now your shirt," Carmody said.

Jack shucked out of the shirt he was wearing, then excused himself to go get another. When he got back to the living room, Carmody resumed his questioning. It seemed to Jack that the detective went on forever. When he glanced at his watch, he saw the whole thing had taken about an hour.

"You both need to come by the police station this afternoon to sign your statements." Carmody fixed Jack with a glare. "At that time, we'll have some more questions for you, Counselor."

Jack's gaze went to Kelly. She stood near him, her arms folded, silent and still as a statue. She was quiet, but he knew better. She was like a tiger, ready to pounce.

When they both heard the detectives' car pull away, Jack picked up his topcoat from the chair where it had been thrown. "I need to get to the office."

"Don't even think about leaving yet," Kelly said, and Jack recognized she had more bite to her voice than usual. "I just ended up with a dead man in my driveway, a man whom you defended in court. A pistol—probably yours and maybe the murder weapon—was found nearby. The detectives are going to try every way possible to tie you to this shooting and whatever criminal activity that man was engaged in. You might stonewall them, but I'm your wife. I want to hear all about it from you—now!"

Jack spread his hands wide. "Kelly, I need to talk with my law partner. Right now, I don't want to share what I learned from Alba with the detectives, and I certainly can't tell you. You have to trust me when I say I'm not a part of any kind of criminal enterprise."

As Jack walked out the door, he knew Kelly was thinking she was married to a man involved in some sort of illegal activity. He longed to tell her what he knew, but he had to make certain he could safely do that—not only for his professional well-being, but because it might endanger them all.

At her office, Kelly was shuffling through what seemed like an endless stack of lab reports when she looked up to see Anna, her nurse, standing in the doorway.

"Safe to come in?"

"Sure," Kelly said. She saw the two cups in Anna's hands and accepted one gratefully. "Thanks. After what I've been through, I'm ready for another cup or three. What a morning!"

She pointed to the chair across the desk from her, and Anna took it. "I didn't know how long you were going to be tied up, so I either rescheduled your patients from this morning or got one of our other physicians to see them."

"Any problems with that?"

"No. Mrs. Lovatto was having a bit of trouble with extra heartbeats, but Dr. Sewell saw her and adjusted her medication. Everything else was pretty routine." Anna took a sip of her coffee. "Tell me all about it. It must have been quite a shock, finding a body in your driveway."

"Yeah. Having your car stop when the rear tire bumps against a corpse is a pretty unforgettable experience." Kelly leaned forward. "One I don't want to go through again."

"The police must have been there for a long time."

Kelly nodded. "I thought the two detectives were never going to let us go. Especially since they found the gun that probably killed the man ... and it's like the one Jack has."

"Did you know the man that your car ... Did you know the dead man?"

"No, but Jack did. He said he'd just represented him on a charge of drug possession." Kelly grimaced at the thought of the conversations ahead of her and her husband, centered around that relationship. "And before you ask any more questions, I think we need to call a halt to this discussion ... at least, for now."

"Fair enough," Anna said. "You're clear until lunch time. And if you need to be gone this afternoon, let me know so I can switch those appointments around."

"Thanks for the reminder. The detective told me to come by the police station to sign my statement this afternoon, so I'll need to leave a bit early." Kelly finished her coffee.

"No problem." Anna picked up Kelly's empty cup and left, only partially closing the office door behind her.

When Jack entered the office, his paralegal, Martin Kirby, and his secretary, Virginia Smith, had their heads together at the front desk, conversing in low tones. Both looked up, but before they could complete their greeting, Jack said, "I'll be in my office. No calls, but when Ainsley is available please tell her I need to see her."

Virginia stopped him. "Mr. Lovelace has been waiting for you." She nodded toward the middle-aged man sitting in the corner of the waiting room. "We explained that you'd been indefinitely detained, but he insisted on waiting."

Herb Lovelace wasn't exactly a platinum-level client, but he and Jack had a sort-of friendship, and his CPA firm threw enough business the lawyer's way to make placating him worthwhile.

"Send him in but interrupt me if he's still in my office when Ainsley is available."

Jack had hardly gotten settled behind his mahogany desk before his visitor came into his office. "Herb, have a seat. I'm sorry to have kept you waiting."

The man who settled into one of the client chairs opposite Jack was about his age, but whereas the lawyer still felt like he could play wide receiver for SMU, Herb's body type trended toward a pear shape. Maybe he was confined to his desk more than Jack.

"I know that you asked me about the legal interpretation of an IRS regulation, and I'm ready to go over that with you. Let me see if I have that citation here."

The next twenty minutes involved Herb listening while Jack told him he was on firm ground with the IRS. "You can tell your client this is well within the statutes."

"Thanks, Jack." Herb hesitated, obviously unsure whether he should ask the next question. "Was this a personal thing that delayed you?"

"I really can't say."

"The reason I asked is because I was talking with Jason Featherstone this morning when I picked up some coffee at Starbuck's, and he noticed a bunch of police cars blocking the alley behind your place."

Before Jack could respond—or think of an appropriate response—Virginia's voice came over the intercom. "Mr. Harbaugh, Miss Serta is here."

"Ask her to come in." Jack rose and offered his hand to Herb. "Sorry, but I need to meet with one of my partners."

Jack ushered Herb out and said good-bye. Ainsley was standing outside the door and nodded as the accountant left. Then she looked at Jack with a question in her eyes.

"Come in and have a seat. Let me just close this door."

Ainsley Serta was the other senior partner of the law firm of Harbaugh and Serta. When they graduated from the same law school and decided to set up a practice together, they had flipped a coin to see whose name would be first on the door, and he won.

Although any lawyer who wants to build a practice pays attention to their dress, Ainsley far exceeded the norm. She always looked as though she were ready to walk down the runway at a fashion show. Of course, in Jack's opinion,

Ainsley would look good in a flour sack. Her beauty was evident from the first glance. Her appearance notwithstanding, opposing lawyers soon learned that behind that glamorous façade was a skilled attorney.

Ainsley was dressed for the season. Her red jacket and skirt and white blouse, accented by a Christmas tree pin, reminded Jack that the holiday was only a few days away. He'd have to check with Kelly to see what they'd be doing as a couple—if he was still alive by then.

"Jack, what's this about? All I know is what you told me when you called this morning. A dead man in your driveway? What's going on?"

"Ainsley, buckle up, because this is going to blow your mind."

"Did you want to get Harry in here as well?"

Harry Chapman was the third lawyer in the firm. He'd graduated from the University of Texas law school and had come highly recommended. He was still "on probation," having joined the firm less than a year ago.

"No, I think this is something I want to talk with you about. If we need to tell Harry about it later, I will."

Ainsley looked puzzled but nodded her assent.

"It began innocently enough," Jack said. "I was at a meeting of my Rotary Club about a month ago when a stranger approached me. The man was tall and thin. Nothing was very remarkable about him except his shock of red hair. He introduced himself, although the name didn't mean anything to me at the time. He said he was just visiting from out of town, so I said 'Welcome,' and started to leave."

"I'm guessing it didn't end there," Ainsley said.

Jack rose and started pacing behind his desk, the way he pictured himself pacing before a jury box. "The man—his name was Farrell—told me a friend in town needed a lawyer. Said it was a matter of getting a traffic stop dismissed. I said we didn't handle that sort of case, but if the friend consulted me in the office, I'd refer him to someone."

"And?"

"He wouldn't take no for an answer. Said it was a slam-dunk case and couldn't understand why I wouldn't do it—especially since the client offered to pay the fee in cash. And it was several times our usual fee."

"So, you finally gave in," Ainsley said.

"Yes, but unfortunately, things didn't end there."

"What happened?"

"The case was indeed a slam-dunk. The policeman who stopped the client did so because he fit the description of a suspect. He found a small amount of marijuana in the car's glove compartment, but there was no cause to search the vehicle. The stop was flawed. It's illegal search and seizure."

"I sense there's more."

"Unfortunately, Eric Alba not only told me about the case, he told me about how he fit into a gun-running outfit that had a big buy coming up. He even told me the date and place. The man thought that, since I was his lawyer, that was covered by privilege."

"A crime that's going to take place? You're bound, as an officer of the court, to report that to the police. Have you?"

Jack shook his head. "He warned me that if I did, his boss would take it out on us both. Today, Alba's corpse turned up in my driveway."

"Wow," Ainsley said. "And I take it you haven't told the police what Alba revealed to you?"

"At first, I hoped things were over and I didn't have to say anything. I figured the higher-ups in this gun-running ring considered Alba disposable, so they got rid of him. But then I started wondering if the placement of his body was meant to send a message to me. Was this their way of telling me that if I talked, the same fate waited for me? If so, they got their message across, loud and clear."

Kelly was looking out her office window when her nurse, Anna, stuck her head around the partially open door. "Doctor, we have a walk-in patient who seems to be in some significant distress, and the other two doctors are tied up with their regular schedules. I could break in on one, but—"

Kelly moved toward the door, grabbing her stethoscope off the desk and shoving it in the pocket of the white coat she wore. "Never mind. It will do me good to stay busy."

The man sat on the edge of the exam table, breathing heavily. His skin was pale, sweat dripping off him. His head hung down so that, if his eyes were open, he'd be looking at the tiled floor. But they weren't open. He seemed to be focusing all his efforts on catching his breath.

"I'm Dr. Harbaugh," Kelly said. "What kind of trouble are you having?"

The man was silent for so long that Kelly thought perhaps he didn't hear her. Finally, he raised his head. "Hurts … Chest hurts … Can't get … my breath."

Kelly turned toward the closed door and said loudly, "Anna."

The door opened almost immediately. When she saw the patient's status, she nodded once.

"Give me a hand, and let's get him lying down. You start oxygen by mask. Take his vital signs, then hook him up to an EKG."

"What about—"

"I'll start an IV and get some blood for stat enzymes and chemistries," Kelly said. "You call 9-1-1."

The man's skin, which started out almost as white as the paper that covered the exam table on which he lay, regained a bit of color with the administration of pure oxygen. After Kelly saw the changes on his EKG, she said to the patient, "Have you had heart trouble before?"

He strained to answer. "No."

"Do you have a doctor?"

He shook his head. "Never ... needed one."

"What medicines do you take? Any drug allergies?"

"Just ... just over-the-counter stuff. No ... allergies."

Kelly turned to Anna as her nurse stepped back into the exam room. "Give him a sixth grain of morphine. I'll put in a call to a cardiologist. We need an ambulance crew to transport him to the hospital stat."

Kelly pulled her cell phone from the pocket of her white coat. Her full attention was on this emergency. She'd deal with Jack's problems later.

Jack leaned across the desk toward his partner. "So that's where I am. And I'm looking for your legal advice about what to do now."

Ainsley Serta frowned. "I thought one of the things we agreed on from the first was that we would discuss any significant case before we accepted it."

"We did, but I thought this was a minor thing, and we could use the fee."

"I don't—"

While Jack talked, he noticed Ainsley rubbing her chin, a habit she had when she was studying evidence and connecting the dots. "I think you're right about Alba's death. It served the dual purpose of getting rid of a weak link and sending you a message. The question now is what you're going to do about it."

"That's what I'm asking you. What's your advice?"

"Obviously, your duty as an officer of the court is to report this," Ainsley said. "I'm not familiar with gun-running. Do you think this will burn itself out?"

"There are people above Alba who regularly finance these illegal firearms exchanges. Sometimes the amount of money that changes hands is in the tens of thousands, and it can go up to six figures." Jack shrugged to ease the tension in his shoulders. "If they have to take a life or two to keep the money flowing, I don't think it will bother them."

"So, you're putting your life in danger if you report this. I see your problem."

"Not all of it." Jack shook his head. "Alba was shot with my gun." He looked at Ainsley. "Someone stole it out of my briefcase—someone who has access to my stuff."

3

In the police parking lot, Kelly had just slid out of her car and slammed the door when she saw Jack's silver BMW come around the corner and pull in. He was closing the door of his car when she walked toward him.

"Looks like we both got here at the same time," he said.

Kelly decided she should probably put her frustrations with Jack aside—at least for now. This wasn't the time or place to start an argument. "I imagine your day was about as bad as mine."

"Maybe worse, but then again, we're comparing apples and oranges." Jack aimed his key fob at his car and clicked to lock it. He took her elbow as they headed for the front door, more guiding than helping her. "Look, I'm sorry if I was short with you this morning. I've had a lot on my mind and finding my client dead in the driveway didn't exactly help me get off to a good start."

Kelly nodded but didn't reply. She could tell Jack was trying to make amends. They could talk more at home. Right now, the best thing she could do was read over her statement, sign it, and get out of here.

They entered the front door of the police station and stopped before a uniformed officer who sat at a chest-high counter, apparently reading from the stapled papers that lay on the countertop.

Out of the corner of her eye, Kelly noticed Jack's mouth open to speak, but he closed it again without a word. She decided that, even though as an attorney he felt he should take the lead in this, he was allowing her to do so. Another point for Jack. Maybe the way he behaved now was influenced by what he saw at the murder site. *I hope.*

"Mr. and Dr. Harbaugh," she said. "Detectives Carmody and Hancock interviewed us this morning. They wanted us to come by to sign statements."

The policeman nodded, picked up the black phone on his desk, and punched in three digits. After a short wait, he said, "The Harbaughs are here. Okay to send them back?"

"Yes." The one-word response and the click that followed carried clearly past the receiver that the policeman held loosely against his ear. He pointed toward a door at the end of the hall. Before Kelly and Jack could turn in that direction, the man's head was down, and he appeared once more to be absorbed in his reading.

They entered a room with desks, chairs, and file cabinets, but no windows. Although she'd never seen one, Kelly figured it was the squad room. It showed evidence of activity over the weekend. Most flat surfaces held empty pizza boxes, partially eaten donuts, empty or partially full Styrofoam cups, and similar debris. The only person in the room was Detective Carmody, who sat at the desk nearest the door through which they entered. In contrast with the rest of the room, his desk was clean and free of debris.

He stood, pulled a chair from nearby, and added it to the straight chair that sat across the desk from him. He gestured at both Kelly and Jack to sit.

She wondered where Detective Hancock was. Her absence must mean this was routine. Kelly relaxed a little.

Carmody opened his top center drawer and withdrew a small stack of paper. He handed each of them a set of two stapled pages, then shoved a couple of Bic pens across the desk. "Read these through. Make any changes that are needed. Then initial the first page, sign the second."

Kelly read through hers, found no need to make any corrections, and scribbled her initials and signature as the detective had instructed. She looked up to find Jack still poring over his. She wanted to ask him what was so important, but his look of total concentration kept her silent.

"Detective Carmody, is there anything else you need from me?" she asked.

"No. But if you and the lawyer here came in the same car, you might want to make yourself comfortable out in the lobby." A fleeting grin crossed the detective's face. "I'm going to have a few questions to ask him in addition to his initial statement."

Kelly remained in her chair. "We're here in separate cars, but I'll be glad to stay in case you want my input."

Carmody looked directly at her when he replied. "Let me be clear, doctor. I want to question your husband a bit more, and perhaps he'll be forthcoming with some of the information if it's given outside your presence." He leaned forward. "I'm sure he'll tell you later what he wants you to know."

Kelly figured the message was clear. She pushed back her chair and headed for the door through which she'd entered.

She paused, thinking about saying something more to Jack, but let it go. She wanted to wait in the lobby for her husband, but Kelly had no idea how long he would be with the detectives. And perhaps he wouldn't want to talk after this was over anyway.

About the time the door to the squad room was closing behind her, she looked back to see Detective Hancock come in from another door in the back of the room. Carmody said something to Jack, then took a tape recorder from his desk drawer.

As she stood on the steps of the police station, Kelly checked the time: five minutes before five. The staff at her clinic would still be there. They might check out to the answering service at five o'clock, but they'd stay as long as there were patients to care for. Perhaps she should call them.

Kelly pulled out her phone and dialed the back number, the one that wouldn't go through the answering service. Her call was picked up after the second ring. She recognized the voice of her nurse.

"Anna, I've finished with my statement and thought I'd head on home. Is everything okay?"

The long pause before the answer gave Kelly an indication of the answer that was on its way. "We've got it covered. There was another walk-in, one who caught his hand in a table saw. He was bleeding pretty severely, but Dr. Sewell took care of him. He may have tendon damage, so after we got the hemorrhage stopped, a surgeon agreed to see him in the ER."

"And did that throw you behind?"

"Well, yes. But we'll get it done. The patients don't mind waiting."

"Are some of them mine?" Kelly asked.

"A couple of yours called in with urgent problems after you left, but…"

Kelly was already walking toward her car. "Never mind. I'll be there in less than five minutes." As she unlocked her Subaru, she wondered when Jack would be finished with the sergeant. She couldn't worry about that now. She had patients to care for.

Out of the corner of his eye, Jack saw Kelly leave the room without saying a word to him. At the same time, Detective Hancock came through the other door and headed for the desk where he sat. The presence of two detectives meant this was going to involve more than just signing his statement, and Carmody's next action confirmed this.

While Hancock dragged over a chair and sat next to Carmody, the detective opened a desk drawer and pulled out a recorder. He checked the batteries and placed the microphone between him and Jack. "You don't mind if I record this, do you?"

Jack looked around and saw that all the other desks in the room were empty. Maybe that was why he hadn't been moved to an interview room. He knew better than to take this as a good sign. Wherever the conversation took place, he'd known it was coming.

When he initially stonewalled the police, Jack had bought himself a little time, but now he needed to speak up. His continued silence would definitely place him outside the law—the law he'd sworn as an officer of the court to obey. On the other hand, telling the police what he knew might cost his safety and even his life.

"Let me give you a Miranda warning," Carmody said. "You have the right to remain silent…"

"I know the words. And I suspect you want me to sign that I've heard and understand them," Jack said. "Let me have the form."

Carmody pulled a printed sheet from the drawer in front of him, shoved it toward Jack, and waited while it was initialed and signed. He looked at the form, nodded once, and put it aside. "Now, Counselor. Is there something more you want to tell us beyond the bare details you gave this morning?"

Jack had thought of nothing except this interview since meeting with his law partner earlier in the day. He had hoped she'd have an answer for him, but after hearing what Jack had to say, she merely reminded him of his duty as an officer of the court.

Although Jack wasn't a Star Trek fan, he'd caught an episode or two. Now he realized this was a classic *Kobayashi Maru* scenario—a situation that there was no way to win. He could either tell the police what he knew, and risk death for himself, his wife, and the people who worked for him, or lie, tell the police he knew nothing more, and violate his oath to uphold the law. The latter meant possible disbarment while the former carried an even more permanent consequence.

Carmody leaned toward the lawyer and spoke a bit louder. "Mr. Harbaugh, did you hear me? Is there anything else you want to tell us?"

"Let me ask you this," he said. "Will you promise me that the only people who hear this recording will be you and your partner?"

"I can't promise that. However, I can say that we'll keep it confidential as long as we can. And that presupposes that, if Alba's murderer ever comes to trial, you'll testify."

"Let's cross that bridge when we come to it," Jack said. "I presume the images from the security cameras showed the vehicle that dumped Alba's body in our driveway and tossed out the pistol—and I wasn't in that vehicle."

"Presume anything you want," the detective said.

"Then, while we're talking hypothetically, let's assume the gun that killed Alba was mine. When the criminalist did a paraffin test to see if I'd fired a gun recently, I'm assuming it was negative. Of course, we all know there are ways around that. And after you get the final results from the pathologist as to Alba's time of death, you'll find I was alone with my wife during that time. I'm sure she will back up my alibi."

Carmody nodded but didn't say anything.

"Anyway, you know that I didn't kill Alba. Although I don't know who murdered him, I probably know why it was done. I think the killing was meant to get rid of a man who talked too much. It was also a way to send a message to me. So, the sooner you find the real murderer and take them out of circulation, the safer I'll feel," Jack said.

"Assuming all that's correct, am I to infer that you have information you'd like to share?"

In for a penny, in for a pound. "Yes. I'll tell you what I know."

Kelly sat in Dr. Cathy Sewell's office, sipping a soft drink and slowly decompressing after more than an hour spent with patients whose complaints ran the gamut from sore throat to abdominal pain that might well lead to an appendectomy if the surgeon concurred.

"Aren't you anxious to get home?" Cathy asked from the chair behind her desk.

Kelly shrugged. "I'm sort of ambivalent. I suppose I should get going, although I honestly don't know when Jack will be home." *Or if he'll be there at all.*

Cathy put down her can of Diet Dr Pepper and looked at Kelly with concern. "Are you still worried because Jack's been a bit distant?"

Kelly grimaced. "Well, it didn't help that we found a corpse in our driveway this morning." She picked up her can but didn't drink. "He seemed a bit better at the police station this afternoon, but I haven't had a chance to talk with him since then. I'm hoping we've just hit a rough patch in our marriage."

Cathy's smile was obviously meant to take the sting from her next remark. "I don't know if I'd call them rough patches. What I've discovered, as I implied earlier, is that every marriage has its ups and downs."

"I understand. I just wanted—" Kelly stopped. What did she want?

That was the question Cathy directed back to her.

Kelly thought about it for several seconds before she answered. "You're the senior physician in a family practice that's going along nicely. Will has transitioned from being a successful lawyer to election as county judge. And, so far as I can tell, your marriage is rock-solid." She shook her head. "I guess I wanted to have the same thing with Jack."

"The only suggestion I can make is what I was told before my own marriage: 'Fight fair, and don't keep score.' And make God a part of everything you do."

Kelly sighed. "That's tough. Jack sort of drifted away from God. But I hope to get him to come back."

Cathy leaned closer. "Let him see that in action through your life. That speaks louder than any words you can use."

Jack explained to the detectives how he came to defend Alba and, in the process, learned more than he should have about the gun ring involved. Then he paused and looked at Carmody. "Alba said he was going to be part of an illegal delivery of firearms several days after his court date." Jack checked the date on his watch. "To be exact, the exchange is scheduled for two in the morning in the alley behind Ellison's Gun Shop, four days from now. As these things go, it may be a small transaction. I don't know. But I suspect an arrest would lead you to the people behind this enterprise. I'm presuming you'll notify the ATF and they can intervene. Right?"

"We can't contact Alcohol, Tobacco, and Firearms just on your say-so. We're going to need something more than that. How about naming names?"

"Alba didn't mention any." Jack felt himself sweating despite the air-conditioning in the room. "He told me about the firearms sale, that's all. And according to the canon of ethics, once he mentioned a crime that's going to be committed, I was bound to report this."

"But you waited until this afternoon to do it. Why not tell us when we were at your house investigating Alba's body in your driveway?" Hancock said.

"I wanted to talk with my law partner first. I know the law, but I needed a second opinion. Maybe she had a way out of my predicament."

"You mean you were hoping to avoid this," Carmody said. "But I guess she didn't have an answer for you."

Jack shook his head. "The moment I tell you what Alba said, it puts my wife, my law partner, and everyone working at my office in danger." Jack swallowed, trying to clear the lump in his throat. "It's apparent to me that

Alba's boss—whoever he or they may be—killed him and dumped the body in my driveway to send a not-so-subtle message that I should keep my mouth shut."

"Suppose that's true," Hancock said. "If you told us what you know, there's nothing more that could be done to you to prevent your talking."

Jack shook his head. "If you think about it, we're still in danger. My death or that of someone close to me would serve as a further object lesson not to cross the group."

"So, you're the victim here?" Carmody shook his head.

"Actually, yes. I'm putting my life and that of others in danger by sharing this information."

"Be that as it may, right now you're still on our list of suspects for killing Alba," Carmody said.

"Why? You think I shot him and invented this story to throw your investigation off the scent?"

"Counselor, we have your gun as the murder weapon. If you didn't do it, maybe you gave it to whoever killed Alba, then cried 'My pistol's been stolen' to throw us off. We've seen that sort of fake before."

"How about the security camera images?" Jack asked. "Did they show who left Alba's body in my driveway?"

"We have a couple of views of the alley that your driveway feeds into. We saw a green, late-model SUV dumping Alba in your driveway and throwing the pistol on the edge of the alley about two hours before your wife discovered the body." Carmody looked down at his notes. "Do you know anyone who drives a green SUV?"

Jack shook his head. "No." *But I'm certainly going to watch out for one now.*

Carmody straightened the stack of papers on his desk. "We'll investigate Alba's murder. We'll also sniff around and see if there's any corroboration to your story about the gun ring. But you're not in the clear on this, so stay where we can find you."

"What about my pistol?" Although Jack had never believed he'd need it since he avoided criminal cases, now he was ready to arm himself.

"We'll need to hang on to it as evidence," Carmody said. "You should know that. If you want to buy another one, just be certain your papers are in order."

You can bet I'll replace it. And I'll be certain to have it within arm's reach 24/7 because I still think I have a bulls-eye on my back. And talking with you just made it larger.

Kelly wasn't certain what to do. This was Thursday, their normal "night out," but today had been anything but normal. It wasn't every day that a body turned up in their driveway—the body of one of Jack's clients. She imagined food would be the farthest thing from her husband's mind, and he probably had no desire to go out. So, should she cook something for them? If Jack was hungry, would he stop for fast food on the way home?

Then again, what if Jack didn't come home? What if Jack's session with the detective, the conversation that transpired after Kelly left, led to his arrest? Was he in jail even now? If that happened, would he phone her? Wasn't a prisoner allowed one call? And if he called, who could she get to act as *his* lawyer? Perhaps she could call his law partner. Or would Jack's first call be to Ainsley anyway?

Cool it, Kelly. You're letting your imagination run away with you. She looked at her watch. It had been well over two hours since she left the police station. She decided she'd wait another fifteen minutes, then call Jack's cell phone. And—

There! She heard the garage door going up, followed by the familiar rumble of Jack's engine. He was home. The anger she'd felt was forgotten, or at least swept aside by simple relief that her husband was home and this terrible day was drawing to a close.

He was barely through the door, still had his topcoat on, when she gave him a hug, followed by a kiss that was more than the usual peck.

"Wow," Jack said. "I guess you're glad to see me."

"It was silly, but I could imagine all sorts of things that might be keeping you from coming home. And you'll have to admit that today hasn't been a usual one."

"Yeah, you're right about that." Jack looked at his watch. "Ready to go?"

"Do you still want to go out? After the day we've had, I wondered if you might want to stay home."

"No," Jack said. "We need this time together more than ever." He took a deep breath. "I need to talk with you."

That didn't sound good. As Kelly hurried to their bedroom to change, she wondered what Jack was about to tell her. She hoped it included an explanation of whatever had made him so jumpy lately. But they were going out, just like a normal Thursday, and that was what she would concentrate on right now. They both needed it.

4

Kelly sat beside Jack in a circular booth at the rear of their favorite restaurant. The booth was situated so that she and her husband could see the rest of the diners. Right now, there were no people nearby. Had Jack asked the woman who seated them for that booth? Kelly hadn't paid attention.

She'd already noted that his demeanor, which had worried her for the past few weeks, seemed better. He was still on edge, but not as much as before. Until tonight, his temper had seemed ready to erupt at any minute, but that had changed. He was more like the normal Jack, the man she married. Maybe something had happened at the police station. Kelly welcomed the change and hoped her husband would explain it.

Once they'd received their drinks and each had ordered, Kelly stirred sweetener into her iced tea. Without looking up, she said, "I trust you're going to tell me what's been bothering you the past few weeks."

Jack took in a long breath and held it for several seconds before letting it out as a sigh. He looked around to be certain they couldn't be overheard. "That's the main reason

I wanted to go out tonight. I've been under a strain. And, unfortunately, I'm afraid it's not over. But I need to let you know where we are, because you may be in danger too."

Kelly felt her pulse quicken. "I don't understand."

"It all began with this guy I met at a Rotary Club meeting. He was visiting from out of town, and I didn't expect to see or hear from him again. But he asked me to help out a friend…"

She sat mesmerized as the story unfolded. Several times she wanted to interrupt the narrative to ask Jack why he took the case, why he waited to finally level with the police, and—if by so doing he made himself a definite target for the gang responsible—why he couldn't simply let things go. But she remained quiet until he finished.

"So, this afternoon you told the police the story about your client and the part he played in distributing guns. Why doesn't that take you off the hook?" she said.

"First, the police still think I'm involved, both in the gun ring and Alba's death, so talking with them didn't really clear me. Second, now that I've told the police what Alba spilled about the forthcoming weapons deal, his bosses—whoever they are—probably will be out to get me."

"Even though you've already shared this information?"

"As an object lesson. You know. 'Don't mess with us, or you'll end up dead.'"

"How long will you be involved?" Kelly asked.

Jack's expression told her the answer before he voiced it. "Until the police no longer consider me a suspect in Alba's murder… and they roll up the gun ring."

The arrival of their meals put a temporary halt to the conversation. They sat in silence and toyed with their food for a while before Kelly said, "Let's go home."

Jack didn't argue. Although he assured the waiter their food was fine, the man insisted on putting their untouched dinners in to-go boxes. When an argument seemed about to follow, Kelly stopped Jack with pressure on his arm. It would be easier to let the waiter prepare the food for them to take home than to tell him it would go right in the trash after they walked in their door.

Kelly walked silently with Jack toward their car, which was parked in the lot adjacent to the restaurant. She was about to buckle her seat belt when she heard the first shot. It took a moment for her to realize what was happening, but when she did, Kelly dropped to the floor of the vehicle and curled herself into the smallest ball possible. She stayed there, on the floorboard in front of the passenger seat, as two more shots rang out. After a period of silence, she heard an engine revving, followed by the squeal of tires.

"Jack?" she called. There was no answer. Kelly lay there for what seemed like an eternity, but it was probably only a few seconds before she cautiously raised her head. "Jack?" she called again.

"I'm ... I'm okay," came a voice from below the open driver's side door. Then, slowly and cautiously, Jack's head emerged into view. "Are you hit?"

"No. Just shaken up." Kelly waited until Jack climbed into the car and closed the door before moving back into the passenger seat herself. "What happened?"

"I thought we might have at least a day of grace before they tried to take me out." He reached over to start the car. "I guess I was wrong."

It was late, but no one was yawning. Jack decided that being on the receiving end of gunfire generated quite a bit of adrenaline. He looked at Kelly, sitting beside him on the sofa in their living room, and wondered if her pulse was still racing as well.

Across from Jack and Kelly sat the two police officers who had responded to Jack's call. One patrolman appeared to be the senior of the two and asked the questions. The other policeman took notes.

"Why didn't you call the police from the restaurant parking lot where this took place?"

"Because someone was shooting at us, and I thought it best to get away from there." Jack could hardly disguise his impatience with the question or, for that matter, the man who asked it.

"Someone took a shot at my husband—three shots, actually—and although you haven't asked, I agree with Jack's decision to get away from there," Kelly said.

Jack held his temper, but just barely. "I talked with Detective Carmody this afternoon and explained what I knew about this case. Why isn't Carmody or his partner here?" *And why do I have to explain everything to two people who know nothing about the background?*

"They'll get our report in the morning, sir," the patrolman said. "I'm sure they'll want to talk with you again."

"I'm sure they will. And I want to talk with them."

"It appears the immediate danger to you has passed." The policeman kept his tone even, but the implications of that statement and the one that followed were hard to miss. "There are no bullet holes in the car—not the door, not anywhere that we could find. We only have your word that something happened."

"I'm sorry the shooter missed," Jack said. "If he'd hit me, you'd have evidence from the ambulance drivers—or the coroner."

"I don't—"

Jack made a gesture of impatience. "We called to report this as soon as we got home. Now will you finish with whatever paperwork you have to complete? I'll talk with Carmody in the morning. Otherwise, there's no reason to go over the story again and again with different people."

"I understand your feelings," the officer said. "Just to be sure, though, would you hit the high points of your story one more time?" He inclined his head toward the other policeman, who looked up from his notebook but said nothing. "I want to make certain our report is accurate."

"I'm an attorney. My client revealed that he was involved in a forthcoming sale of illegal weapons. I gave the information I had to the detectives, although by so doing I realized I might be inviting the criminals to kill me. And that's what happened tonight."

"Did you see your assailant?"

"I saw the glint of something metallic a few cars away in the parking lot. I decided I'd rather look silly by going to the ground for no reason than maintaining my dignity but ending up dead from a gunshot. That's why I sort of ducked behind the open car door. When I heard the first shot, I slid all the way under my car and stayed there until I heard the other vehicle pull away."

The policeman turned to Kelly. "And you?"

"When the first gunshot sounded, and I recognized what was happening, I dove to the floor of the car and curled into a ball. I wanted to stay down and thought the engine block might give me some protection. When the shooting stopped, I called out to Jack."

"You didn't go to him?"

She shook her head. "And expose myself in case the gunman decided to shoot me? I guess I might have, but when I shouted to Jack he said he was okay."

"I think that's all we need." The lead policeman rose, and the other officer followed suit. "I'll make certain a copy of this report gets to Detective Carmody in the morning. In the meantime, just so you know we're not totally dismissing your story, there's another team combing the scene for clues. If the gun was a rifle or a semi-automatic pistol, we may find some of the ejected cartridges or other evidence of the shooting."

"Will that help you identify the shooter?" Kelly asked.

"Not really." Both officers turned toward the door. "But it would add credence to your story."

Kelly's residency training had included a number of occasions when she'd worked through the night, leaving her weary as she saw her patients the next morning. But none of those involved someone shooting at her, so her feelings on Friday morning were new to her. And she didn't ever want to experience them again.

She yawned when Anna put the day's schedule and a cup of coffee on Kelly's desk. "Thank you," Kelly managed to say once her jaw relaxed back to its normal position.

"Are you sure you're okay to work today. I imagine we can reschedule—"

"Thanks, but no more rescheduling." Kelly stifled another yawn. One way or another, she needed to get through this. If Jack could go to work this morning, she could too.

"Okay. When you have time, Dr. Roberts would like a few words with you."

"Sure. Send her in now before I get started."

Betty Roberts had joined the family practice group just over a year ago. She'd moved here from Dallas after her husband divorced her, filling a vacancy left when one of the other doctors retired to settle down and raise her family. With no children and no siblings, her parents both dead, Betty said there was nothing to tie her down. She wanted something to fill the void in her life and decided a move here was a good way to get a fresh start. When she found out the position was open, Betty grabbed it.

Kelly had never felt especially close to Betty. Maybe it was the age difference. Betty Roberts was in her late fifties, while both Cathy and Kelly were almost twenty years younger. The older doctor had never sought out Kelly like this, so she couldn't help wondering what was going on.

"May I come in?" Betty tapped on the door frame and paused, waiting for the okay before entering Kelly's office.

Today, as on most days, Betty's silver hair—which she said she declined to dye—was faultlessly styled. Her only make-up was a faint darkening of her lips by lip gloss. A spotless knee-length white lab coat covered her slacks and tee shirt, with a stethoscope peeking out of the right-hand side pocket.

Kelly pointed to the chairs across from her desk. "Have a seat, Betty."

"I won't be here that long," she said. "I just wanted to say that if you need anything—anything at all—don't hesitate to ask me."

"I appreciate that."

"You know," Betty said, "sometimes people say things, but they don't really mean them. But I do." She pursed her lips, seemed to think a bit, and then went on. "I don't have anything or anyone to go home to, so if I can help take some of your professional burden off you, anything to help you keep your family together, I want to do it."

Kelly had never heard Betty say this much in the time she'd been here. She was still formulating a response when the older doctor spoke again.

"I know you've been having trouble at home." She raised her hand. "No, I haven't heard you say anything, but it's fairly obvious. Whatever the stressor—and finding a body in your driveway can't have helped—it can either split a marriage or draw you closer to your husband. So, if you need me to cover your patients or do anything else for you ... well, let me know."

With that, Betty turned and walked out, leaving Kelly to ponder her words. Was she offering to Kelly what she wished someone had done for her? The younger doctor didn't know—but she appreciated it.

Jack looked at the two people who sat across his desk—Martin Kirby, the middle-aged paralegal, and Virginia Smith, the older woman who acted as secretary and office manager. Along with the three lawyers, they constituted the bulk of the legal staff of Harbaugh and Serta. Two receptionist/typists were still at the front desk, and he'd tell them later.

But these people, along with Ainsley Serta and Harry Chapman, were most likely to face any further retribution.

He wanted to share his current situation with them, not so much asking for their help as warning them they might be injured or killed as collateral damage if Alba's boss—whoever he or they might be—took measures to shut him up permanently.

Jack looked to his left where Harry sat, a somewhat puzzled look on his face. On the other side, Ainsley had relocated her chair, placing it at the end of Jack's desk. He raised his eyebrows, but she made a palms-up gesture with her right hand, as though to say, "You have the floor."

He took a deep breath. "I've told Ainsley about all this. Harry, you need to hear it too, and I think Martin and Virginia should know the full story as well." Jack then proceeded to outline how he came to defend Alba, the information he'd learned from the man (despite his efforts to stop his client from telling him) and why he thought Alba's murder served a dual purpose.

"I've told the police what I know," he concluded. "They're looking into it, but I've already had one attempt on my life. Unfortunately, you're at risk as well. I wanted you all to know, so you can take precautions. And if you think your continuing here is too dangerous…" He left his sentence unfinished.

Harry glanced first at Jack, then at Ainsley. "I don't know if that offer to leave includes me, but if it does, I'm staying."

Jack nodded at Ainsley who said, "Harry, we're glad you're staying." Her eyes then rested on the two senior employees. "If either of you feels threatened, feel free to tell us. You can leave with no hard feelings. We'll make certain you get a good recommendation."

Jack looked at the two people across the desk from him. "You may be thinking, 'I didn't sign up for this.' If that's the case, feel free to resign. I won't blame you. Don't worry about two weeks' notice, either. All I ask is that you don't spread this information around."

After a rather extended silence, Martin smoothed his tie against his wrinkle-free white shirt, cleared his throat, and raised a hand.

Martin was once a high school teacher, and Jack decided the hand-raising was part of an ingrained habit. The man had been a successful teacher of high school civics, but he grew tired of it. Martin had decided he was too old to go to law school. Instead, he decided to pursue the paralegal profession, for which Jack was grateful. His presence was almost like having another attorney on board.

Jack pointed at Martin, who lowered his hand. "What's on your mind?"

"Do you have any idea who the mastermind is behind this . . . I don't know what to call it. I guess it's a gunrunning ring. Do you or the police have any clue about them?"

"Not really," Jack said. "I've done a bit of research on the subject, and despite the fact that most people picture a gang that deals in stolen firearms, most illegal weapons flow through licensed gun dealers, either through diversion of large numbers of guns or 'straw man' purchases of smaller lots."

Virginia, looking cool and calm as always, spoke up. "So, the police or whatever agency they cooperate with only have to check out licensed gun dealers? That shouldn't take long."

Jack shook his head. "Gun transactions like this don't respect boundaries—city limits, state lines, whatever. There are about 125,000 licensed firearms dealers in the country, so the law enforcement agencies can't check them all. I think what the police will be looking for is not just the smaller fish, but the person bankrolling the ring in which Alba was one link. There's often one person behind something like this, and that's who they're after."

Ainsley brought the conversation back to the original purpose of the meeting. "Now you know the situation. Jack has already told me about this, and I'm staying. But it may be dangerous to keep working here." She looked at Martin and Virginia. "What are you going to do?"

"I'm not going to run," Virginia said. "Not at my age, and certainly not from threats like this. If I was spooked by dangerous situations, I wouldn't have lasted as a legal secretary for so many years."

"And this is certainly more exciting than teaching high school civics," said Martin. He chuckled. "One of my friends who's going to law school at night just said he's considering dropping out. He's decided maybe he doesn't want a law degree."

"Did he saw why?" Virginia asked.

"He said being an attorney was a boring profession."

5

Kelly heard the garage door close, followed in less than a minute by Jack walking into the bedroom where she stood. "Tough day?"

"About like yours, I'd imagine."

She looked at him, and they communicated with a glance the same way many married couples do. They said, almost simultaneously, "Let's order in."

"Pizza?" Jack asked.

"Fine," Kelly said. "I'll change clothes while you call in the order."

She dressed in jeans and a tee shirt and slid her bare feet into loafers. When Jack walked back into the room, she smiled at him. "Mission accomplished?"

He stretched out on the bed and folded his arms under his head. "Just the way you like it. I even asked for extra mushrooms."

Kelly perched on the other side of the bed. "Jack, why didn't you tell me about the problem with that man when you were handling it?"

Jack closed his eyes. "Do you tell me about every case you have?"

"No, but I share about the ones that are of interest, the patients whose problems are complex or potentially lethal."

He shook his head. "But, aside from HIPAA restrictions—which you skirt when it comes to talking with me—you don't have any prohibitions on sharing information you've learned. Lawyers do."

"Jack, I don't identify my patients by name when I talk with you," she said. "And the outcome of those cases doesn't put me or my family in danger. If they did, I'd tell you."

Jack opened his eyes and looked at her. "When I first took on this case, I figured it was an easy way to bring in a few dollars for the practice. Sure, it was outside my usual area of practice, but I'm an attorney. I've passed the bar exam. It certainly wasn't beyond my capability to defend someone on a minor drug charge, especially one I was assured was a 'slam-dunk.' I took a look at the circumstances, thought I could get the man off, and decided to run with it."

"And then..."

"And then he told me some things I didn't want or need to hear. What I learned involved a crime about to be committed, so privilege was not only waived, but as an officer of the court I had a duty to share it with law enforcement."

Kelly reached over and took his hand. "But you put not just your life but the lives of other people in jeopardy."

"Unfortunately, that was the choice I had to make. Today I told the staff at the office the situation, including an apology for letting this happen. But no one wanted out." He looked up at her. "Now you know all about the mess I'm in. You're in the line of fire too. Do you..." He left the question hanging.

She grinned, although it was a bit forced. "I didn't know that 'for better or worse' would include someone shooting at me when I promised to stick by you, but I'm prepared to be your partner for the duration."

On Saturday morning, Kelly turned off the alarm and eased out of bed. Jack stirred, but she gently put her hand on his shoulder. "Go back to sleep. You don't have to get up, but this is my weekend to work."

He sat up in bed, rubbing his eyes. "I don't want you in the car by yourself. I'll drive you and pick you up after you're through."

"No, I don't plan to change my routine, no matter what Alba's boss—whoever he is—tries to do. I'm not going to cower, even after finding a body in my driveway."

Jack swung his feet to the floor. "Didn't those shots at our car scare you? Do you know how serious this is?"

"I know, but you're not going to change my mind." She leaned over and kissed him. "I'll call you later this morning when I have a chance. For now, try to get some rest."

"Will you be through at noon today?"

"Depends on how busy we are, and whether I have to go by the hospital to see a consultation before I go home. We can decide about lunch later."

Kelly whizzed through preparing a buttered, toasted bagel and a travel mug full of coffee, then headed out the door with what passed for breakfast. She climbed into her Subaru Legacy and started it. Then she noticed the fuel gauge showed almost empty. Kelly had driven with that much on a number of occasions, although she knew it drove Jack crazy. But with the weekend coming up and her on call, she wondered if that was smart. Maybe she could take Jack's car, and he could fill this one for her.

She hurried back into the house and found Jack in the kitchen, pouring coffee into a mug.

"Problem?" he asked.

"Not a big one." She explained the situation. "Would you have time to fill my car while I take yours?"

"Sure."

Not a word about letting the gas gauge get low. Maybe Jack really was going to act like the man she'd married. "Thanks. I'll give you a call when I see how things are going today."

She hung her car keys on the rack by the door from the kitchen to the garage and took the ones to Jack's BMW. Kelly had driven it a few times, but usually she took her car. The cold hit her as soon as she walked into the garage and raised the door, and she shrugged deeper into her heavy coat. When she started the engine, she noticed Jack's fuel gauge showed almost full. She wasn't surprised. He was always prepared for an emergency.

Kelly couldn't help checking that the driveway was clear. No, no bodies this morning. The light snow that had fallen just a couple of days ago had mostly melted, even though the temperature was still in the forties, and she had no problem backing out into the alley.

Because it was early on a Saturday morning, the traffic wasn't too bad. Her mind was drifting a bit when she saw a rental truck coming from her left on the intersecting street. The light was green in her direction, but she slowed anyway as she approached the intersection. *Always assume every driver is an idiot, and you won't often be disappointed.*

Her car was in the intersection, her eye on the traffic light, when she felt a sudden hard jolt. Her vision was blocked by the deployment of the air bag, but she could feel the vehicle sliding sideways. Kelly fought for control, but the BMW didn't respond. The car moved to the right, then stopped with another jolt. She realized it must have hit the wall of the Kroger's store that sat on one corner of the intersection.

She took stock of herself and was a bit surprised she had escaped major injury. Kelly had pushed the seat forward from the position where Jack had left it—after all, he was over six feet tall—and she initially felt trapped by the inflated air bag. But after a few seconds, the bag partially deflated and she was able to wriggle free. However, when she tried to open the driver's side door, she found it was crushed inward and immobile. She crawled across to the passenger side, but that door wouldn't open either. When she looked through the shattered glass of the passenger window, she could see why. The right side of the car had slammed against a wall. Kelly looked around and realized she was trapped inside the car.

Kelly took a deep breath and fought the panic building inside of her. She reached for her cell phone. It wasn't on the seat where she'd put it. *Don't panic.* Surely, someone would have called 9-1-1 by now. The first responders would include people with the tools to get her free. She just had to wait.

And then she smelled the gasoline.

Jack disagreed with Kelly's decision to drive herself to and from work today. He had wanted to shield her from the mess he'd created, but she'd have none of it. He hadn't been able to stop the gunshots aimed at him less than 48 hours ago, but he hoped that was the last of it. Maybe he was naïve. Surely, though, the police would soon locate the person bankrolling the gun operation. The exchange of weapons for money would take place soon. Maybe the authorities would not only be able to stop it, but round up those responsible. If that happened, he could breathe easier.

He rinsed his coffee cup and put it in the dishwasher. He was trying to decide whether to run it or wait a bit longer when his phone rang. Since Jack didn't handle criminal law (until the Alba case) he didn't expect any calls from clients at home. He lifted the receiver but heard only a dial tone. Then he realized the call was on his cell phone. When he checked caller ID, it showed an unlisted number. Some telemarketer probably. But just before it rolled over to voicemail, Jack decided to answer.

"Mr. Harbaugh, this is Tom Carmody."

Jack furrowed his brow. The name sounded familiar, but he didn't—Wait, that was one of the detectives with whom he'd dealt. Had they swooped down on the gunrunning ring already? He started to respond, but Carmody didn't give him a chance.

"Your wife has been in a car accident. She's in the hospital right now—Collins Memorial. I'd like you to get down here as soon as possible."

"What—"

"I'll explain when I see you. Come to the emergency entrance. My partner will meet you there." Then the detective hung up.

Kelly's recollection was fuzzy. She remembered leaving the house... She squeezed her eyes shut and forced her memory to bring more to the surface. Finally, she remembered the crash and the sensation like a huge boulder colliding with her car. She tried to remember the details but could only bring up fragments—being trapped, smelling fumes, and then flames followed by an explosion. Her last memory was of being strapped to a gurney.

At that point she must have blacked out completely, because the next thing she knew she'd awakened in a hospital room with two beds. The curtain around the other was pulled back, and a glance showed she didn't have a roommate. Gingerly, Kelly took stock of her situation. She ached all over but had no burns or bandages of which she was aware. Nothing restricted the motion of her arms or legs, no casts or braces. There was no oxygen running, no IVs in her arms. Despite a distinct feeling that the crash was followed by a fire and explosion, she seemed to have escaped serious injury. Then why was she in the hospital now, apparently alone in this room?

"Are you awake?"

The voice came from the far end of the room, and when Kelly looked that way she saw a man in a wrinkled suit sitting in a chair drawn up next to the door. Rising stiffly, like the tin man who had been left out in the rain, he moved toward her. As the man drew nearer, she recognized one of the detectives who'd responded to the call about a dead body in her driveway. Had that only been a few days ago? She'd seen him again at the police station when she signed his statement. What was his name? It danced at the edge of her memory, but she couldn't retrieve it.

"Doctor, I'm Detective Carmody. Do you remember me?"

"I...I remember the face, but I couldn't recall your name."

The detective stopped at her bedside. He leaned over but didn't touch her. "I've called your husband. My partner, Detective Hancock, is going to meet him at the emergency entrance. She'll bring him here, and then we can talk about what to do next."

"What happened to me? Why am I here?"

Carmody lowered his voice, although the door was closed and there was no one else in the room. He spoke slowly, apparently to make sure he was getting through. "You were driving your husband's car. A rental truck T-boned you. The driver fled the scene on foot. You were trapped in your car. The fire department and EMTs arrived quickly. They used the jaws of life to get you out just before the gas tank caught fire and exploded."

"But I seem all right."

"They pulled you out just seconds before the car went up. Since you were essentially unconscious, the EMT's strapped you to a gurney and headed for the hospital. You escaped with just a few bumps and bruises … possibly a concussion. I'd flagged your name and husband's, as well as your address and the plates of both your vehicles, so I got a call when the accident was reported. I spoke by radio to the ambulance attendants when they were on their way here. I arranged for them to bypass the ER and take you directly to this room.

"A doctor hasn't seen me?"

"The EMTs didn't think you were seriously hurt, but I had a doctor who owed me a favor examine you. You may not remember any of this, because you were still coming around, but you escaped serious injury."

"Then if I'm okay, why am I still here?"

"Yes, why?" Her husband Jack stood in the doorway with Detective Hancock right behind him.

"Now that you've arrived, Counselor, we can discuss my suggestion."

The drive to the hospital had been a nightmare for Jack. He had grabbed the keys to Kelly's car off the hook, but when he started the car, he checked the fuel gauge. Now only did it show empty, but the icon showing a need for fuel was lit. That's when he recalled why she wanted to trade cars with him. Well, there was no time to put gasoline in the car now.

All the way to the hospital, Jack watched the needle bounce below the empty level and prayed he wouldn't run out of gas halfway there. Fortunately, the streets were clear, although some snow still lingered on grassy patches, so he was able to make good time.

Kelly had a staff parking sticker on her windshield, but Jack didn't want to take the time to park in that lot. Instead, he pulled into the emergency room driveway, parked in a space reserved for patients, and hurried through the sliding glass doors and toward the registration desk. Before he could approach the woman sitting there, a black lady stepped toward him and held up a badge case.

She kept her voice soft, although no one was within earshot. "Mr. Harbaugh, I'm Detective Hancock. We met when my partner and I investigated the body in your driveway, and again when you were at the station on Thursday."

Jack nodded. "I remember. But where's my wife? What happened? Detective Carmody called and—"

Hancock put a finger to her lips. "Your wife was in a car accident, but she's fine. I'll take you to her now."

Without waiting for his response, Hancock led the way down a couple of corridors, looking over her shoulder twice

to make certain no one was following. They took an elevator labeled "staff only" and rode to the third floor of the
hospital. After they exited, the detective took Jack past a
glass-fronted area that was full of bassinets and newborns
to a room at the very end of the hall. "Your wife is in here,
and my partner is with her. Go ahead in. I'll stay outside
the door to keep anyone from entering."

"Why—"

"He'll explain everything."

Jack tapped lightly on the door, then entered without
waiting for an answer. Kelly was in the bed farthest from
the door. Carmody was beside her. There was no one else
in the room.

Kelly was asking, "Why am I still here?"

She was okay. Jack heaved a sigh of relief. "Yes, why?"

The detective appeared unruffled. "Now that you've
arrived, Counselor, let's discuss my suggestion."

Jack closed the distance to Kelly. Hesitantly, as though
she'd break, he hugged and kissed her. When she hugged
him back, Jack increased his pressure, until she finally said,
"Hon, I need to breathe."

He released her and stepped back. "Detective, what
about the crash? Is my wife okay? And if so, why is she still
here? Fill me in. Fill both of us in."

"I'll explain. Just let me—"

Kelly showed her impatience with a wave. "Answer my
husband's question. And start by telling us where we are
in this hospital. I'm on the staff, and this doesn't look like
most of the rooms I've seen."

Carmody nodded. "This is an overflow room in a wing
of the hospital occupied by newborns and mothers. At present, in addition to my partner and me, the only ones who

know you're here are the EMTs who brought you to the hospital and the doctor I asked to examine you. They've all been sworn to secrecy."

"Why?" Jack asked.

"Counselor, it was your car that was T-boned. It was your car that burned after the gas tank exploded. The ambulance brought someone here, and so far as anyone knows, that someone was you. I propose we put your name on the patient roster, then stake out your room to see whether someone tries to finish the job."

"I presume, then, that you'll want me assigned to a room that's easily accessible to whoever comes for me."

"Yes," Carmody said. "And you'll need to stay in that room all the time, although there'll be a policeman concealed in there as well."

"Why can't I just lay low at home?" Jack asked.

"If anyone sees you, even catches a glimpse of you through the window at your house, they'll finish the job they started. No, the best scenario has you staying right here."

Jack looked the detective in the eye. "What I'm hearing is that I'm not really a suspect anymore. Now I'm bait!"

6

Kelly had kept silent while Carmody explained his plan, but eventually she decided to inject a bit of reality into the conversation. "Detective, if Jack sustained injuries in the crash, he'd have gone through the ER and to the ICU. And those rooms have windows, so the nurses can keep an eye on the patients. After all, they're 'critical,' which is what the 'C' in ICU stands for."

"I realize that, but an ICU room wouldn't work as well for our purposes. But suppose the person behind the gun ring—or, more likely, whoever they send—isn't as familiar with the hospital as you are. I'd suggest we at least give my suggestion a try. We put him in a regular room for a day or so—say he's being held for observation for internal injuries. If that doesn't draw another attempt on him, Jack can go home, and we go back to what we had before."

"Which was 'watch your back,'" Kelly said.

Jack furrowed his brow. "I think the detective's right. It's at least worth a try."

Kelly tried one more time. "But, honey, they're using you to bait a trap."

"Not just me," Jack said. "Do you realize that whoever wants to silence me might come after you instead? He could kidnap you and use you as bait."

She hadn't thought of that. "But—"

"Jack will be safe with me or another officer on guard here. We'll have an unmarked car and a couple of officers watching you as well." Seeing Kelly's look, he continued. "Both you and Jack will be as safe as we can make you. This is a perfect opportunity to draw out the person we're seeking."

Jack looked at her. "I think we need to do this."

Kelly finally gave in. She accepted the car keys from Jack and gave him a final hug and kiss. *At least there's a chance this will work.* She found her car where Jack had left it. She wasn't happy with what Detective Carmody had arranged. Actually, she wasn't happy with Jack being used for bait. Nevertheless, she'd finally agreed it might be the best maneuver.

Just as she opened the door of her Subaru, she recalled where she'd been headed when the truck had T-boned Jack's car. She was on call this weekend. Kelly looked in her pockets and purse for her cell phone, but it wasn't there. It must still be on the floorboard of his car . . . unless it had been destroyed in the accident or the fire that followed.

Under the circumstances, Kelly wondered if it wouldn't be a good idea to trade call with one of her colleagues. She could call Cathy Sewell, who was the senior member of the group, but she had a vague recollection that Cathy and her husband were going out of town this weekend. Then she thought of Betty Roberts. She'd offered to help. And she was a divorcee, so she should have no family obligations that might keep her from stepping in.

Kelly closed the car door and walked back toward the hospital. She avoided the busy admitting and triage area of the emergency room, going directly to the room where the staff took their breaks. She picked up the phone there, only to realize that all her phone numbers were stored in her cell phone. With a sigh, she dialed the hospital operator and finally managed to convince her that she really was Dr. Kelly Harbaugh, and that she needed the home number for Dr. Betty Roberts.

"I can give you that," the operator said, "but Dr. Roberts isn't home."

Kelly frowned. "And you know this how?"

"She just called in from the ER and asked me to try to locate you. It seems you didn't answer at your home or your cell phone, and…"

Kelly hung up with the operator still talking. She rose from the chair where she sat, then stopped when she saw Betty coming toward her. "Oh, Betty. I'm so sorry I've—." She paused. How could she tell her colleague why she hadn't answered without betraying the scenario the detectives had set up to catch whoever was after Jack? But this was Betty. She'd offered just days ago to help. Well, Kelly could use some help right now. Who better to share her feelings with than her grandmotherly colleague?

Kelly looked around to make certain they were alone in the breakroom. "Betty, please sit down for a minute. If you still want to help, I need to unload on you. This has been a terrible day for me so far, and I'm worried about Jack."

Betty smiled and took the seat on the sofa that Kelly indicated. Her gray eyes conveyed genuine sympathy, as did her tone. "Tell me all about it."

Jack looked around the new room into which he'd been moved. It was on a different floor than the out-of-the-way one where he'd met Detectives Carmody and Hancock. There had been a good bit of cloak-and-dagger sneaking around to get him here. In some way he still didn't understand, he was now registered as a patient in this room.

The public story was pretty much as Carmody had laid it out. Jack was driving his car when the rental truck crashed into it. He was extracted from the burning car just before it exploded and rushed here by ambulance. Jack was being held for observation to rule out any internal injuries. There was an "absolutely no visitors" sign on his door. And Detective Carmody would be sitting behind the drawn curtain surrounding the other bed.

"Can I watch television?" Jack asked after he was settled in.

Carmody shook his head. "It's better if you don't. We don't want any sound coming from this room."

"And the other logistics?"

"The supervisor on this floor knows a little about what's going on. Three nurses, hand-picked for their discretion, will be responsible for this room twenty-four hours a day. They'll maintain a chart on you, check your vital signs, bring you a tray like you were a real patient."

"Can they be—"

"I know what you're going to ask," Carmody said. "And yes, they can be trusted. The doctor who checked over your wife will be here regularly to look in on you. We've vetted everyone who knows what we're doing, and we're trying to keep that number as small as possible."

Jack didn't ask about the food. He could already imagine the lime gelatin coming his way, but that was a small price to pay. Besides, he needed to lose a few pounds.

"Any other questions?"

"You'll have someone watching my wife? And there'll be a police presence here to protect me?" Jack became aware that he hadn't replaced his pistol, the one the police were still holding as evidence. At this point, all he could do was depend on the promises he'd received.

"We'll be here around the clock."

"But not Hancock. Right? My wife is already unhappy enough with my being used for bait like a staked goat."

Carmody made a calming gesture. "I'll take the first watch. Then Corporal Peters will take over. He's one of our best, and he knows how to keep his mouth shut about this assignment."

"And the undercover officers covering my wife?"

"Our best. They'll keep their mouths shut. Don't worry. Just put yourself in our hands."

Kelly talked with Betty for almost an hour. She wasn't sure whether the peace she felt at the end of that time was because her colleague insisted they pray together, or simply the calming effect of time passing. Maybe it was the benefit of sharing with another person, or knowing she wasn't alone. Whatever the cause, she felt better when she walked out of the ER. Betty had said she'd be glad to cover for Kelly this weekend and made her promise to call if there was anything more she could do.

Kelly looked around as she exited the hospital but couldn't identify the police who were her protectors. Were they even there? All she could do was depend on Carmody. Her life, and that of her husband, were now in the detective's hands.

As Kelly opened the door of her car, she knew there were two things she needed to do immediately—fill her gas tank and retrieve her cell phone. The first was easily accomplished, although she did have a moment when the car sputtered, causing her own fuel pump—her heart—to beat rapidly. Kelly kept an uneasy eye on the fuel gauge until she pulled into a station and started filling the tank. When she saw the amount of gasoline that it took to fill her car, she realized that it literally had been running on fumes.

One problem down, one to go, and this one proved to be more of a challenge. She had no idea where Jack's car had been taken after the accident. *No problem. I'll just call police headquarters and ask...* Oh! She couldn't do that. She had no cell phone. Kelly watched for a phone booth, and soon discovered they were a thing of the past. She finally convinced the teenager behind the counter of a small convenience store to let her use the phone there. After two sessions on hold and one disconnect, Kelly was finally able to get the address of the facility where cars were taken when picked up by a wrecker.

When she got there, she discovered a sign informing her that the yard closed at noon on Saturday. Her watch showed it was half past twelve. Kelly wanted to cry. If she had her cell phone, she could call and see if someone would take pity on her. Of course, if she had her cell phone, she wouldn't need access to Jack's wrecked car anyway.

Kelly hadn't decided what she'd do next when the door of the shack on the other side of the wire fence opened and a young man emerged. He wore wrinkled jeans with holes at the knees, a tee shirt that had seen better days, and athletic shoes that were the color of dirt. Both his forearms bore tattoos, although she couldn't make out what they said. She was ready to get in her car and pull away when he yelled at her.

"Hey, did you need something?"

Yes, she needed something. She needed her cell phone, and the only way to get it was to get past that locked gate. Kelly took a deep breath, then said, "Yes. I need to get to my husband's car. He was involved in a wreck earlier today, and my cell phone is still in there."

As the man approached the gate, Kelly got a good look at the tattoos. On his right upper arm was a shield-like design featuring crossed arrows and the words, "De oppresso liber." She'd never seen one like that before and had no idea what the Latin meant. She had to admit, though, that it was better than the death's heads and swastikas she was afraid she'd see.

"Is your husband okay?" the young man said as he reached through the wire of the gate, pulled the chain toward him, and unlocked the padlock that held it closed.

"He's … he's going to be okay," Kelly said. "I guess you get asked this all the time, but what does—"

"Oh, the Latin motto on my tattoo. It means 'To set the oppressed free.' Everybody in my squad got them."

"Your squad?"

"I served in the Army, Special Forces. That was our motto. But I realized there was another way to set the oppressed free, one that was better for me. That's why I didn't re-up. Instead, I'm now a student at the seminary."

He held out his left arm. The tattoo there was of an upright sword, with a Bible behind it. "The sword of the Spirit," he explained. The gate swung open and he beckoned her inside. "Why don't I help you find that car? And I'll be certain to pray for both you and your husband tonight."

Jack had only been lying in bed for a few hours, and already he could feel himself going stir-crazy. A late luncheon tray had been delivered shortly after he got to his new room. The meal wasn't bad, but consuming hospital food was no substitute for sitting down at his own kitchen table and eating what his wife cooked. Jack made a mental note to never, ever complain about Kelly's cooking in the future, even if she served him lime gelatin for dessert. That is, assuming he eventually got out of here.

A light series of taps on the door brought Carmody to his feet. He reached beneath his coat and drew a wicked-looking pistol that had apparently been resting in a shoulder holster. The door swung slowly open, and a man eased through. His complexion was a shade darker than Jack's, but his features were Caucasian. He wore jeans and a sports shirt, and his shoes were almost new Air Jordans. Ignoring the man in the bed, he addressed the detective, his hands held waist-high, a badge wallet in the left one. "Corporal Peters."

Carmody returned his gun to the holster under his left arm. "Now I recognize you. Do you understand how this is going to work?"

Peters stowed the badge. "Yes, sir. I stay in here, guard the subject, and deal with anyone who comes in other than the nurse." For the first time, he looked at Jack. Then he turned back to the detective. "Have I got that right?"

Carmody nodded. He looked at his watch. "I had to leave home sort of suddenly. Give me a couple of hours, then I'll relieve you."

The man shook his head. "Why don't I take it until tomorrow morning?"

"What about supper?"

"I'm good. We can probably wrangle some extra coffee when the nurse brings his evening meal. I'll be fine."

Carmody nodded. "I won't argue with you." With that, the detective slipped out the door.

Jack rose from the bed and held out his hand. "Jack Harbaugh."

The policeman eased over toward him, his head partly turned toward the now closed door. "Dave Peters."

"And you're going to protect me?" Jack heard how that sounded, so he added, "I don't mean that I doubt you. I just want to be sure I understand how this works."

Dave lifted the tail of his shirt to show Jack a holstered snub-nose revolver. He gestured toward the bed farthest from the door. "I promise to stay awake tonight, so when you're ready, try to get some sleep."

Kelly's breath caught when she rounded a corner of the yard and came on the silver BMW she'd been driving. Jack's car was totally trashed. The side window glass was starred and shattered, the entire driver's side was caved in, and the rear of the car—the area over the gas tank—was covered with charred paint. She could see the ragged metal around the door where the firemen had used mechanical means to get her out of the car. Just a few more seconds in that death-trap, and she probably would have ended up in the morgue.

"Are you okay?"

The young man with the tattoos had one hand lightly on her elbow, and he increased his pressure, probably thinking he was going to have to hold her up.

"No, I'll be fine. I was just thinking"

"I know," he said. "It's a wonder your husband came out of that alive."

"My husband…" She quickly recovered. "Yes. He was fortunate."

"We can look, but it's possible that your husband's cell phone might have burned," the young man said. "Let me check for you. There's no need in you getting your clothes dirty." He looked down at what he wore. "I always go home looking like I've rolled around in dirt and grease."

It took him a few moments and several tries before he managed to wriggle inside the car. After a couple of minutes, time when Kelly felt her hope dying within her, he reappeared, holding a cell phone aloft. "Here it is. It had slid under the passenger seat."

Kelly took the phone and saw that it was still on, although its battery had almost fully discharged. She checked and found it still worked!

"You've been so very helpful," she said. "I know you were leaving when I showed up here trying to get this. I really appreciate your staying." Her hand moved toward the purse that she had slung over her left shoulder. "Let me—"

The young man held up his hand, palm outward. "That's not necessary. Just glad I could be of assistance." He started walking with her back toward where she had left her car outside the fence. "And I'll pray for your husband."

Kelly nodded. "Thanks." *Me, too.*

The windows of the room where Jack had been stashed were covered by closed venetian blinds. He couldn't see the outside but was able to get some idea by the amount of daylight that seeped through the slats. When would someone come? Or would they come at all? Would he and Kelly go through this, only to find that no one took the bait?

At every sound outside his door, Jack tensed. Corporal Peters sat quietly in the chair partially shielded by the curtain around the other bed. He was situated so that when someone entered, their focus would be on the occupant of the bed in the farthest reaches of the room.

Jack tried to engage Peters in conversation, but the policeman put his forefinger to his lips. After a couple of tries, Jack wondered what he could do to relieve the monotony. He considered the TV, but quickly found that closed captioning wasn't available, and he didn't like watching programs with the sound muted. He had nothing to read other than the Gideon Bible in the bedside table. That wasn't Jack's idea of reading matter, and even if it were, he wondered if he'd be able to concentrate on the words.

If Kelly were here, she'd undoubtedly open the Bible and start reading it. She probably would use the time and opportunity to pray. But Jack couldn't focus, even if he wanted to.

Maybe he should call his wife. Her cell phone might not have survived the crash—he didn't recall seeing her with it when she was here earlier—but he could always call their landline. But when he raised the cell phone to his face, the patrolman next to the door saw him and vigorously shook his head no.

Jack gave the man a puzzled look and received in return another shake of his head, followed by a finger to the lips, followed by hands over the ears. Jack nodded. If he were truly injured, he wouldn't be talking on the phone. How about a text? Through several attempts and gestures, he managed to convince the policeman what he wanted to do.

The response was a nod and a repetition of the hands to the lips. Do it but be quiet.

When Jack pulled his cell phone from his pocket and opened the message app, he realized he couldn't send a text to his landline—only to another cell phone. And since he had no idea if Kelly had her cell or it was lost in the crash, she might not get the message he sent. Since he had nothing to lose, Jack decided to send a text and hope she got it.

First, he needed to find out if his own device had power. He squinted in the room's dim light and saw that his phone battery had less than ten percent of its capacity. And he had no way to recharge it. Would that be enough? Then Jack looked at the bars for signal strength. The indicator for his iPhone showed one bar.

Jack paused with his fingers over the keys of his phone. What should he say? What could he communicate to his wife? He'd love to hear her voice, knowing she'd have encouraging words for him, and sending a text message was a poor substitute. Finally, after several stops and starts, Jack tapped out a simple message. "Love U. Miss U. Don't worry." He hesitated for a moment and added, "Pray for me." Then he pressed the arrow to send it into cyberspace.

7

Kelly didn't sleep well on Saturday night. Some of it was soreness from the car accident—apparently the day afterward brought some areas of pain that weren't obvious at first. And some of it, perhaps most of her insomnia, was due to Jack's absence.

Several times she came partially awake and reached out to feel Jack's comforting presence next to her, only to remember that he wasn't there. She tried to go back to sleep each time, only to repeat the process after an hour or less. Finally, she rolled out of bed, threw on a robe, and scuffed on well-worn slippers to the kitchen, where she flipped the switch on the coffee maker.

Surprisingly, Kelly gave very little thought to the danger she was in. Rather, her concern was for her husband. The detective's scheme that had Jack acting as bait didn't exactly thrill her. She was surprised that her husband had accepted it. Maybe he felt guilty for involving her in this mess. Perhaps Jack wanted to ingratiate himself with the police, offering himself as a sacrifice in order to trap the person behind the gunrunning ring Alba had mentioned. No matter the cause, Jack was in danger. And at present his safety was protected only by the element of surprise and a policeman with a pistol.

Kelly wanted to talk with him, see him—no, she wanted to bring him home. She wanted this situation never to have come up in the first place. But it was what it was, and she and her husband would have to get through it.

She didn't know how long she sat there, drinking coffee, staring out the kitchen window into the darkness. She closed her eyes to think about the problem, and when she opened them Kelly realized she must have fallen asleep. She looked out the window and saw that the world was tinged with the red and yellow hues of approaching dawn.

Kelly remembered plugging her cell phone into the charger last evening in the kitchen and never picking it up again. When she got around to picking it up this morning, she noted the display showed an unread message. The text was from Jack. She read it and smiled. Then she bowed her head and did just as he'd asked—she prayed for him.

Now it was time to get moving. She finished her coffee, took the mug to the sink to rinse it, and considered her next move. If Jack were hospitalized, wouldn't she want to be at his side constantly? She had no experience with situations like this as a family member, but she did from the standpoint of a physician. At some point the staff—either a doctor or nurse—would tell Kelly she should go home and get some rest. If that were the case, though, she should be headed back to the hospital again.

Once she made up her mind, Kelly dressed quickly. She heated an English muffin, buttered and ate it, washing it down with some orange juice and another cup of coffee. When she slid into her car, the dashboard clock showed 7:15. She wondered if Carmody spent the night or shared the duty with another policeman. Either way, she assumed he'd show up at the hospital soon.

Kelly was pleased to see that the last vestiges of the snow had melted. She started to back out of her driveway but had to stop as an unfamiliar car, a tan Dodge, drove by slowly. The driver of the car looked straight ahead, but the passenger—a younger, dark-complexioned man—directed his gaze toward the open garage door. Was that the team watching her? Or was it someone assessing the chance of kidnapping her in order to draw Jack into their trap?

She tried to put those thoughts aside. It was time to head for the hospital. After that ... Well, she'd see.

Jack finally eased into a troubled sleep sometime after midnight. The room was still dark when he was awakened by the opening of the door. He heard a brief exchange, the voices too low and the conversation too brief for Jack to hear what they were saying. He lay still, his eyes closed, wondering why the undercover officer allowed an intruder to enter.

His pulse raced as footsteps approached the bed, muffled by crepe-soled shoes. When the person reached his bedside, Jack decided he had to act. His bare hands were no match for whatever weapon the intruder planned to use, but he had to take whatever defensive measures he could.

Just as he sat up in bed, the light over his head went on and a pleasant female voice spoke. "Mr. Harbaugh, I'm glad to see you're awake. I brought you some breakfast. And there's a thermos jug of coffee and a couple of extra cups if the policeman guarding you wants some."

Jack raked his tousled hair out of his eyes and ran a hand over his chin, feeling the rasp of day-old whiskers. "Who ... Who are you?"

"I'm Carolyn, one of the nurses on this ward. And don't worry, there are only four of us who know a bit about what's going on, and we've all been told to keep mum about it."

He looked at his wrist and saw that it was after six o'clock in the morning. Then he looked at the breakfast tray, surprised by his hunger.

"I expected a liquid diet or something like that. But this looks great. Thank you."

Carolyn nodded and headed for the door, where Peters continued to stand, one hand on the knob. He let her out, then glanced at Jack, who now sat on the side of the bed. "Enjoy your breakfast."

Jack pointed to the tray. "Do you—"

Peters looked at his watch. "Carmody will relieve me in another half hour or so, and I can eat then. But I'll take a cup of that coffee if you have enough."

Jack chewed and swallowed the food Carolyn had brought, pondering as he ate. When he'd heard someone approach in the darkened room, he'd automatically assumed Peters had either failed to do his job or was somehow in the employ of the people involved in the gunrunning operation. Was it because he didn't know the policeman as well as he did Detective Carmody?

After Jack had spoken with the detectives and laid out his involvement, he'd assumed he could trust them. But could he? Right now, Jack was essentially trapped in this hospital room with Carmody or Peters. Maybe the detective was right, and this gave the best chance to catch the people responsible for trying to kill him, but didn't it also make it easier for someone to take advantage of the situation? Was Peters reliable—reliable enough to guard him during the night-time hours?

And what about Detective Hancock? Was she trustworthy? Then there were more police Carmody said he'd brought in to protect Kelly. How did Jack know they were doing their jobs? What if whoever was behind this decided to kidnap her and use her as a pawn to get him.

In addition, there were the nurses who knew at least some of what was going on. Jack's safety depended on these people, any one of whom could leak his location. The more he thought about it, the more people he realized were involved in what Carmody had described as a small operation. Could he depend on the MICU crew who brought him here to keep quiet? And what about the doctor Carmody had asked to examine Kelly before they made the switch?

He glanced sideways at Peters, who had resumed his position by the door. The policeman was enjoying his coffee, apparently at ease. Was Jack letting his paranoia run wild? Or was he reaching a valid conclusion? He realized that, when all was said and done, he really couldn't trust anyone.

When she parked her car at the hospital, Kelly looked around for the tan Dodge she presumed contained the plainclothesmen assigned to guard her. Either they were very good at concealment, or Carmody had lied about police protection. No matter. She'd gotten through the night, and now she was back here, anxious to see her husband.

Kelly walked in, only to realize she didn't know Jack's room number. Yesterday, she'd taken the keys to her car from Jack and headed for where he'd told her it was parked.

She hadn't thought to ask him where his new room would be. Now she had no idea where to go.

She approached an older lady staffing the Information Desk. "I'm Dr. Kelly Harbaugh. My husband Jack is a patient. I rushed here yesterday to see him but didn't make a note of the room number." She smiled sweetly. "Can you help me?"

The woman tapped a few keys on the computer in front of her. "Yes, he's shown as a patient, but the name has a notation that he's not to have any visitors."

"Well, I'm not exactly a visitor, am I? I'm his wife. And a physician on the staff. I just need the room number."

The argument went on for another five minutes, and Kelly thought she was going to have to take her plea to the administrator. Finally, the lady gave in. She extended a small slip of paper with the room number. "If I get in trouble for giving this out, I'm going to tell them how this went down."

"Thank you." As Kelly walked away, she wondered how the hospital might punish the volunteer—take away her pink coat? *Hey, don't be hard on her. She was just doing her job.* As Kelly entered one of the elevators and pressed a button, she made a mental note to apologize later. That is, assuming she wasn't making funeral arrangements for her husband … or dead herself.

Kelly found the room easily. The time was wrong—visiting hours were later—but her face was familiar to several of the nurses, even if they couldn't recall her name. Maybe she should have worn her white coat to help identify her. She tapped on the closed door, opened it, and was immediately confronted by a determined man pointing a gun at her.

She stopped and held her empty hands away from her. Her eyes fixed on the pistol in the man's hand, she quickly said, "I'm Jack Harbaugh's wife. Ask him to vouch for me."

"She's okay, Peters."

Kelly hurried across the room to Jack, and their embrace was long. She couldn't believe that only a few days ago she thought the magic had gone out of her marriage. Confessing to the police what Alba had told him might have put Jack's life in danger from whoever ran the firearms ring, but it also appeared to have restored their relationship.

"Kelly, the man over there who almost shot you is Corporal Peters." Jack indicated the policeman, who had re-holstered his pistol. "If we continue this much longer, I suppose we should arrange some sort of password for you so that no one gets shot by mistake."

The policeman didn't seem at all fazed by the situation. He nodded. "Mrs. Harbaugh."

Before Jack or Kelly could say anything, there was a series of light taps on the door. Peters opened it and Detective Carmody entered. How did he do that without the policeman so much as making a move for his pistol? She knew Jack had been joking about a password, but was there one?

Carmody looked at Peters. "Any problems?"

"None. Do you want me back here at the same time?"

"You can report a bit later today." He ran his fingers through his hair. "We'll give this one more day. If there's no activity by tomorrow morning, you can go back to your normal duty."

Peters shrugged. "I'm happy to do this as long as you want me to, sir."

"Come back about four o'clock today. Same signal as before," Carmody said. "Three light taps on the door."

So there really is a passcode. The detective could have told me that. It would have saved me a near heart attack.

Before Carmody settled himself in the chair near the door, Jack stared at the detective with laser focus. "Come here. I want to look you in the eye when I ask a question."

"I already know the question." The detective stopped next to the bed on which Jack and Kelly sat. "Nothing happened last night, so are we going to continue this? You heard me tell Peters, 'Let's give it one more day.' If there's no activity tonight, I'll let you leave here tomorrow morning."

"Am I still a suspect in Alba's death?"

Carmody sighed. "You were probably right. Whoever stole your gun shot Alba and dumped his body in your driveway as a warning. And we don't think it was you."

"What about ballistics?" Jack asked.

"He was killed with your gun. But there are no prints on the pistol. Not even yours. Even the cartridges remaining in the cylinder had been wiped clean."

"And the person who lifted the gun from my briefcase?"

Carmody shrugged. "We're looking at people who might have taken it from your briefcase, but that boils down to almost anyone."

"Have you done anything about the gun buy that's going down in a few days?" Kelly asked.

"Will you have people staked out to catch the ones involved?" Jack said.

"We haven't decided." Carmody looked back at the door before he continued. "If we just scoop up the little fish, the ring will regroup and continue. We'd prefer to know who's behind these deals and take them off the table."

"And that's why you have me here as bait," Jack said. "But if that's the case, how are you going to get the word out where I am?"

"We don't need to advertise. If the people we want are looking for you, they'll find you."

Carmody turned and started back toward the chair near the door but turned back when Kelly spoke.

"Won't the visitor you're hoping for come at night?"

"Unfortunately, we don't know when—or if—anyone will come. The best we can do—"

"I know," Jack said. "Bait the trap and be ready."

Kelly finally decided that nothing she could say or do was likely to change Carmody's mind. He was steadfast in his determination to keep his trap set for at least one more day, which meant that Jack was stuck here. She sat and took Jack's hand in hers.

"I suppose I should go," Kelly whispered to her husband. "We don't want the bad guys to hear us talking."

He nodded his understanding. They parted with a kiss, and she made her way to the door of the room. Before leaving, Kelly made sure she recalled the sequence of knocks that would let whoever was standing guard know a friend was about to enter. She didn't feel like facing a drawn gun again.

"I'll be back this afternoon," she whispered to Carmody. He nodded.

In the hall, Kelly paused outside the door and thought about things she could do while at the hospital. Betty

Roberts had agreed to take her calls this weekend. She had no consultations to occupy her or patients to see. Finally, she decided the best way to add to the illusion of a husband who was stable but still hospitalized for observation was for her to do the few things she might ordinarily do on a Saturday. And that meant leaving the hospital.

She decided to use the staff elevator, which was closer. Just as she reached it, a man approached from the other direction. "Aren't you Dr. Harbaugh?"

"Yes?" Kelly looked carefully at the man, trying to decide if she knew him. A knee-length white coat covered his Polo shirt and pressed khakis. She glanced at the name embroidered over his breast pocket but didn't recognize it. He was tall and thin, clean-shaven, with a shock of somewhat unruly red hair.

"We haven't met, although I know who you are. I was wondering…" He inclined his head away from the elevator and toward the open doorway opposite. "Can we step over there to have a bit of privacy?"

Kelly followed him to the empty room. "What is it?"

His voice, previously quiet and smooth, took on a hard edge. He gripped her arm with one hand, while pulling a pistol from beneath his belt with the other. "I know your husband is in this hospital. I thought I'd have to nose around some until I found out exactly where, but you can lead me straight to him." He motioned with the barrel of the handgun. "Let's do that. Now!"

8

Kelly moved down the hall of the hospital. The fake doctor leaned into her and murmured nonsense phrases, all the while keeping a firm grip on her right upper arm. To those around her, she was walking with a colleague. He'd tucked the pistol into his belt, out-of-sight, but his free right hand hovered near his waist, ready for him to push the white coat aside and draw in a single motion.

Kelly stopped before the door of Jack's room. She raised her free hand. "I ... I'd better tap on the door."

"No. I want this to be a surprise."

"We always let the patient know we're coming. It's second nature with health professionals." It was obvious the man's plan was to shoot Jack, then her. Maybe this way, she could warn Carmody of what was about to happen.

Kelly tapped with the back of her hand, her knuckles barely making a sound. Tap, tap, tap.

She waited a couple of seconds and knocked again. Tap-tap, tap-tap, tap-tap.

The man pushed Kelly aside. "I know Morse code. You're trying to send an SOS to whoever's in there. It's a trap, isn't it?" The man hesitated for a second, his hand reaching for his waist-band, before turning and vanishing down the hall.

Kelly leaned against the door, her heart pounding. After a couple of deep breaths, she rapped more loudly on the door—three quick taps. When the door opened, Carmody stood there with a drawn gun, but this time she was glad to see him.

Jack saw the expression on his wife's face and covered the distance from his bed to where Kelly stood in a few seconds. He embraced her. "What's wrong?"

Carmody stuck his head into the hall. When he discovered no one outside who wasn't supposed to be there, he closed the door and joined Kelly and Jack. "Tell me about it. It sounded like you were trying to send me an SOS. I was about to jerk the door open, but it sounded as though you were interrupted."

Kelly told him about the red-haired man and the pistol he carried.

"Was there something on the end of the barrel?" the detective asked.

"Yes. Some sort of extension."

"Probably a noise suppressor—what you'd call a silencer. I imagine he planned to finish off Jack and get away with no one the wiser. Then when he saw you, he simply figured he'd kill two birds with one stone."

"Your trap almost worked, but he was too smart," Jack said.

Carmody nodded. "Unfortunately." He looked at Kelly. "It's not your fault, Dr. Harbaugh."

"Does that description mean anything to either of you?" she said.

Jack rubbed his chin. "Tall, thin man with red hair? Could be the guy who approached me at the Rotary Club and arranged for me to defend Alba. I'd guess he was middle-management of some sort. He probably tried to frame me for Alba's death, then arranged for the crash that was supposed to kill me. And when that didn't work, he tried to finish off the job while I was alone in a hospital room."

Kelly turned to the detective. "There's no use in continuing the charade now, is there?"

Carmody holstered the pistol he still held. "No, I guess Mr. Harbaugh can go home."

"Just like that?" Jack said. "Do you have a Plan B? If they tried to take me out here, they'll try again."

"I'll ask the two detectives who've been following your wife to continue shadowing you for a while. Other than that—"

"I know," Jack said. "Watch your back."

Jack grabbed the shaving kit and the fresh shirt and set of underwear that Kelly had brought him after his first night in the hospital. He stuffed everything into the sack the hospital provided and was ready to go. Kelly pulled her car into the hospital's port-cochere. Then Jack, accompanied by Carmody, stepped out of the double doors, tossed his belongings into the back seat, and buckled his seat belt.

"Can we do something about getting me some wheels?" Jack said as Kelly pulled away from the hospital. "My car is sort of bunged up."

Kelly didn't take her eyes off the road. "You can talk with your insurance agent tomorrow morning, but I can tell you, after I saw your car at the impound lot, I'm pretty sure it's totaled."

She glanced into the rearview mirror. There was no sign of the tan Dodge whose two occupants were supposed to protect her.

Jack looked at his watch. "If you don't mind taking the time, why don't we go to the airport?"

This time Kelly looked at him and frowned. "Why?"

"Because all the car rental agencies are out there."

Kelly insisted on staying nearby while Jack arranged to rent a dark blue Camry. Then they headed for home, a two-car caravan—three if you counted the unseen detective car.

After they reached home, Jack said, "Let's order in tonight."

"Is that safe? With someone gunning for you?"

"Come on, Kelly. We can't live our lives in a bubble."

"Give me a minute." Kelly went to the front door, opened it, walked out on the porch, then returned. "I think we can chance it. Why don't I order pizza from the place where we usually get it?"

"I'm not sure what you saw out front, but sure." Jack started in the direction of the bathroom. "I'm going to shave, take a shower, and put on some clean clothes."

Kelly picked up the phone. "I'll call in the order. Then I want to get something out of the garage."

"What?"

"Something I should have thought of before this. Something we may need."

By the time Jack had taken a long hot shower, shaved, and put on clean clothes, he heard the doorbell. "I'll get it." He reached into his pocket to make certain he'd transferred his wallet and money clip. Although the snow that fell just a few days ago had all melted, it was still cold out.

He planned to tip the pizza delivery man (or woman) a bit extra for getting out in the brisk weather.

Jack expected the person at the door to be the one delivering the pizza Kelly had ordered. Instead, he saw a familiar person waiting outside, blowing on his hands to keep them warm. Jack eased the door open. "Harry! I didn't expect to see you."

Harry Chapman nodded once. "Can I come in, Jack?"

"Sure." Jack stepped away from the door, then motioned the junior lawyer in his group into the living room. "What brings you out this evening?"

Harry ran his hand through his blond hair, a gesture Jack had already learned meant the man was a bit nervous. He and Ainsley hadn't specifically discussed the matter, but Jack was certain that in a couple more weeks, when Harry had completed a year as an employee, they'd sit down with him and suggest he find another position elsewhere. He simply hadn't shown them he had what it took to be a successful attorney—certainly not in their practice.

"What can I do for you?" Jack asked again.

"I think it's what I can do for you," the younger lawyer said. "I'll give you a choice. Will you go peacefully, or do I have to stage a break-in before I shoot you?" With that, Harry reached into the pocket of his coat, pulled out a pistol, and pointed it at Jack.

Kelly looked up when she heard the doorbell. She was in the garage and had just found what she was seeking. Jack could answer the door. Kelly gingerly removed the object she wanted from a shelf in the garage. There was a box behind it, and she took some of its contents and added them to what she held in her hand.

As she entered the kitchen, she heard an unfamiliar voice coming from the living room. But it didn't sound like the pizza delivery guy. Then she heard Jack's voice, and its tone was one of puzzlement. She nodded to herself and moved softly toward the living room to see what was up.

Just before she reached the door into that room, she heard the man ask Jack if he wanted to go peacefully. If not, he was going to shoot her husband. Kelly started to pull out her cell phone and call the police, but quickly rejected that idea. There was no time. This was up to her.

She slipped out of her shoes. Then Kelly took a deep breath, said a silent prayer, and tiptoed on stocking feet to the entrance of the living room. She peeked around the doorframe and saw a younger, blond man holding a pistol on her husband. Kelly quickly pulled her head back.

"I don't understand," Jack was saying. "What are you doing?"

"Cleaning things up."

Jack stared at Harry. It wasn't possible that this lawyer, his associate, was standing there holding a pistol on him. Then he thought of Kelly. Would she blunder back into the room? Would Harry shoot her? Right now, keeping the man talking seemed the best course of action.

"It was obvious to me as soon as I settled in that a nickel-and-dime practice with you and Ainsley wouldn't generate the kind of income I'd imagined. But then I had a chance to make a lot more money on the side. Unfortunately, things went awry. And the person I told to clean them up didn't do it. So, I'm taking care of it myself."

"What do you mean by 'things went awry?'"

Harry shook his head as he recalled the situation. "Remember the day Farrell approached you at the Rotary Club and insisted you defend Alba?"

"Farrell?"

"The red-headed man."

"Oh, yeah."

"Well, you had planned to take me with you to the meeting that day, but I was under the weather. Farrell had orders to approach the lawyer he met there, but he forgot the name. He was supposed to ask me about representing Alba. I'd demur at first, just as you did, but finally accept. It was perfect... but then it wasn't."

"So, my involvement wasn't planned?"

A wry smile painted Harry's face but was gone as quickly as it came. "No. Farrell killed Alba to keep him from talking, as he was ordered to do. I thought you'd get the message, but you went to the police anyway. Then Farrell was supposed to take care of you, but he failed. So, it all comes down to me."

Surely, Kelly had called the police by now. Was there something in the house she could use for a weapon? She couldn't go for his gun—the police still had it, and he hadn't purchased a replacement. And was it safe for Kelly to go up against Harry anyway? Maybe it was best for Kelly to hide. Perhaps at some point he'd be able to end the confrontation by wresting the pistol away from his attacker. It seemed to be his only chance.

"Why gunrunning? How did you get into it?"

Harry shook his head. "Jack, I know that in detective stories, the criminal always explains everything before the hero's rescued, but that isn't going to happen here." He motioned toward the front door with the barrel of his pistol. "Get moving. We're going for a little ride in my car." His colleague snickered. "A one-way ride."

Before either of them could move, Kelly's voice sounded loud and clear as she stepped around the partially closed door to the kitchen. "I don't think so. Drop your gun and kick it away." Kelly's command was punctuated by the distinctive *chuk-chuk* of a shell being jacked into the chamber of a shotgun.

Harry turned toward Kelly but didn't relinquish his pistol. "Have you ever pulled the trigger on a shotgun like that? It has quite a kick." He took a step toward Kelly. "I don't think you'll shoot, and if you do, you'll miss. Why don't you drop your gun and come over here?"

As Jack watched, Kelly turned the barrel of the shotgun she held upward and fired a shot into the ceiling, followed almost immediately by the sound as she jacked another shell into the chamber. "This is a ten-gauge. I can't miss at this range. And if you'll notice, when I fired that warning shot, Jack moved aside so the scatter from my next discharge wouldn't hit him. This is your last warning. Drop your pistol and kick it over here. In three … two … one…"

Harry dropped his pistol and kicked it away as she'd instructed. Then he held his hands out to his side.

"Jack, get all the way behind me to completely clear my line of fire."

Jack did as his wife asked. "Have you called 9-1-1?"

Without turning her head, she said, "That's why I looked outside before we ordered the pizza. Turn on the porch light, step outside, and wave your arms toward the tan car parked at the end of the block. I'm guessing the police in there heard the gunshot and will get the message."

To Kelly, it seemed like hours, but it was probably more like five minutes before Jack returned, accompanied by two people—a man and a woman—who held pistols. She didn't recognize them, and for a minute she worried that she might have misinterpreted the situation. Were they really the police? Or were they working with the man she held at bay?

The woman answered the unasked question. She held up a badge wallet with the hand that wasn't holding a pistol. "Police. Put down the shotgun and step back."

"Come on. Didn't Carmody tell you who we were when you were assigned to protect us?"

"My partner and I are holding pistols. We have everything under control. Put your shotgun down. Then we can sort out who's who."

Kelly gently laid the shotgun on the floor. Eventually, she and Jack were able to identify themselves and relate what had gone on. Shortly thereafter, Chapman was handcuffed and handed over to the patrolmen who had arrived, apparently in response to a radio message sent by the undercover police from the tan Dodge before they headed for the house.

Kelly took a deep breath. "For a while, I didn't think there were really detectives following us. Then I saw your car parked down the block and recalled seeing it behind me a couple of times before that."

"We're not detectives," said the female officer, whose name turned out to be Hicks. "We're police officers, assigned to this plainclothes detail."

"But we'd certainly like to be promoted to detective," said her partner with a smile.

Kelly started to reply, but before she could do so Detectives Carmody and Hancock walked through the door. "There's someone else pulling up out front," Carmody said.

Jack frowned. He left the room, returning in a few minutes with a box containing the pizza they'd ordered. "I'd forgotten about this."

Carmody dismissed the plainclothes detail. "Report to me in the morning." Then he smiled. "You did a nice job, and I'll see that it goes on your record."

Eventually, Kelly and Jack got through recounting the whole story from start to finish. Both detectives listened intently, interrupting sparingly to ask a question or request a clarification. Finally, they left, after arranging for Jack and Kelly to sign their statements at police headquarters the next day.

"Still hungry?" Jack asked.

"I know I shouldn't be, but I am. Let me heat up this pizza."

Kelly and Jack went to the kitchen, where she put the pizza in the oven while Jack set two places at the table with plates, napkins, and glasses.

"I suppose the shotgun was a surprise," Kelly said.

"To say the least. Not that I'm not glad you had it, but where did you get it? And how did you learn to shoot?"

Kelly shrugged. "After I graduated from med school, my father took me aside and gave me a Mossberg 10-gauge automatic. He insisted that I go with him to the range several times, because I needed to get used to firing a weapon like that."

"But—"

"I know. When I moved here, I put it on a top shelf of my closet—unloaded, of course—and forgot about it. When I went from my apartment to this house after we were married, I stored it in the garage, along with a box of shells. I intended to get rid of it, but I forgot."

"What made you think of it now?"

Kelly shrugged. "When the police confiscated your gun, I decided that it wouldn't hurt to have it available." She opened the oven door and pronounced the pizza warm enough to eat. "I guess my dad was right. The shotgun did come in handy. Sorry about the hole in the ceiling, though."

"Honey, you can shoot holes in every wall of this house if it means saving my life."

It had been a long and sleepless night for both Jack and Kelly, but things seemed to be winding down. They had promised the detectives that they'd come to the station today to finalize and sign their statements. "Want to ride together?" Kelly asked.

"Do you think we need to do that for security?" Jack said. "Because otherwise, I suspect you'll be needing your wheels to go to the hospital, while I ought to have transportation to my office, the courthouse, and wherever I need to go today."

After a bit of back-and-forth, they decided to take separate cars. But Kelly had to admit she felt a bit more secure as Jack's rental car almost rode her back bumper all the way to the police station.

Detectives Carmody and Hancock met them and guided them to an interview room where they could review and sign their individual statements. When they were finished, they took seats in the squad room across from Carmody, with Detective Hancock occupying the chair at the side of the desk.

"Will you be able to charge Chapman?" Kelly asked.

"We're holding him for attempted murder, but we only have your word against his that he's guilty of that."

"He hasn't admitted anything?"

"Nope. He's asked for a lawyer," Carmody replied. "Other than that, he's stood mute."

"Does he have counsel?" Jack asked.

"No, but at least he's not trying to defend himself."

"Do you think he'll cut a deal?" Kelly asked.

"We'll try to get him to give up the person who financed this whole thing, in return for some kind of a deal. But we'll have to see how it goes."

Before either Kelly or Jack could respond, Carmody's cell phone rang. He looked at the display and excused himself.

Kelly, probably sensing that Hancock was the more sympathetic of the two detectives, asked, "Is Jack safe now?"

"Not yet, but my guess is that we'll have the case nailed down soon."

"So, I'm no longer a suspect," Jack said. He made it a statement, but it really seemed to be a question.

"I can answer that." Carmody strode back into the room, stowing his cell in a pocket as he walked. "That was the watch commander. Your red-headed man, whose name was Farrell, was found dead in an alley several blocks away. He'd been shot execution-style by a 9 mm semiautomatic handgun, the same type of pistol we recovered when we arrested Chapman."

"What does that mean?" Jack asked.

"If we can match bullets from Chapman's gun, we've got a murder charge to levy against him."

"He more or less admitted that he took care of Farrell himself," Jack said. "Now I understand what he meant."

"The way I put it together, this was a small operation. Chapman was upper management. Farrell was a middleman, charged with running it. Alba was supposed to pick up the guns, but he was involved in that traffic stop. He had to get that dismissed so he'd be free to carry out the gun deal."

"So..."

"Farrell fouled up by thinking you were the lawyer he should ask to defend Alba. Eventually, Chapman lifted your gun out of your briefcase and told Farrell to kill Alba because he let the cat out of the bag. And he wanted Alba's body left in your driveway as an object lesson for you."

"Was Farrell the guy who tried to kill me in a car accident?"

Carmody nodded. "When that didn't work, he tried to finish the job by getting you at the hospital...just as I thought he would. After he failed at that, Chapman decided to take over, which he started by killing Farrell. Then he was going to get rid of you."

"Will the gun deal still go down on Tuesday?"

"No, that deal's dead. On the other hand, I imagine that eventually Chapman will give us the information we need to roll up the whole ring. I've already called the ATF— Alcohol, Tobacco, and Firearms—who want to question our friend too."

"So, is Jack safe now?" Kelly asked.

"From police prosecution? He's been cleared. From revenge by the higher-ups in the gun ring? I'm not sure. Maybe a bit longer. Depends on how it goes with Chapman."

"But for now?"

Carmody and Hancock responded in concert. "Watch your back."

On Monday morning, Kelly's mind was busy with the things she needed to tell her colleagues. At this moment, Jack was probably doing the same thing at his office. She headed for the break room and poured a mug of coffee, which would be her third of the day. Kelly anticipated that she'd consume even more before the sun set.

She decided that Cathy Sewell's office was a good place to gather everyone. Cathy was at her desk, a cup of tea at her elbow, going through some lab forms. Kelly tapped on the doorframe. "Got a minute?"

Cathy smiled and gestured her colleague in. "Sure. What's up?"

Before Kelly sat, she said, "Is Betty Roberts in yet? She should probably hear this as well."

When she learned Betty hadn't yet come in, Kelly started to say she'd wait until she could bring all the doctors up to speed. Then she decided Cathy needed to know now. She'd tell Betty later. Kelly pulled out a chair, set down her mug, and began. "This started with my husband Jack agreeing to defend what was represented to him as a violation stemming from a minor traffic stop."

To her credit, as Kelly related her narrative, Cathy didn't interrupt with questions. She sipped hot tea, but other than that her gaze never left her colleague.

Finally, Kelly said, "So that's where we are. Most of the danger is past, but there's still the problem that someone was bankrolling Harry Chapman. And if that's the case, he may come after Jack to close the loop."

"You needn't worry." Both women looked up to see Betty Roberts standing in the doorway.

"How long have you been there, Betty?" Kelly asked.

Betty came all the way into the office and took the other chair next to Kelly. "I heard you telling Cathy where things stand. As you recall, you told me most of the story this weekend when I agreed to cover for you." She looked at Cathy, then back to Kelly. "And I want to assure both of you that this is totally over. There'll be no retribution from the person providing the financing for Harry's gun ring ... because that was me."

9

Jack stirred his iced tea and looked around. Because it was early, there weren't many other diners in the restaurant. He'd asked for seating in a rear circular booth, with no one near them. It was a perfect location for him to talk with Kelly about the latest in this crazy scenario that was, hopefully, coming to an end.

"I intended to call you all day, but no sooner had I told Ainsley what had gone on and we'd planned how to take up the slack left by Harry's absence than a client came in needing both of us. And I barely came up for air until time to leave the office."

Kelly covered her husband's hand with her own. "What will you do now that Harry's no longer a part of your practice?"

"We'd both pretty well decided that we were going to part ways with him after he completed his first year with us. Ainsley has an appointment with a woman who's due to graduate from law school in a few weeks and is interested in joining the practice." He lifted his glass and drank. "What about you? What did Cathy and Betty have to say when you told them about our adventures?"

"I told Cathy what was going on. Betty showed up at the end of my session, but she knew most of it. Then she proceeded to floor both of us with some additional news."

The conversation stopped as the salads were served. Kelly picked up her fork, but Jack stopped her. "Don't you dare take a bite and start chewing until you tell me about this news."

Kelly put down her fork and folded her hands. "To begin with, Betty didn't move here after her husband divorced her. Actually, her husband died. She decided she had too many memories in that town, so she looked around for a new location. About that time, she was contacted by her nephew, telling her of an opening for a physician in town. Because she thought it would be good to be in the same place as her nephew, she looked into it."

"And that's pertinent because—"

"Because the nephew was your associate, Harry Chapman," Kelly said. "After she moved here, he requested that Betty stake him with ten thousand dollars of the life insurance proceeds she received."

"Why did he need the money?"

"Betty asked that same question, but all Harry would tell her was that it was a one-time investment, and she'd get her money back with interest."

Jack looked around to make certain there were no listening ears nearby. "Did she ever find out what the money was for?"

"She finally gave him the money, but she didn't learn the rest of the story until Harry called her last evening from the police station."

"Wow," Jack said. "So, she was the person behind all this."

"Only in the sense that she gave Harry the money. He thought he'd start small, and with the profits from this transaction he could enlarge the operation until he had a nice little sideline income. Betty didn't know anything about it until she got that call."

The waiter came by and asked if there was something wrong with the salads. Jack assured him they were fine, and as soon as the man was out of earshot, said, "So we don't really have anything further to fear? All the people involved are either dead or in custody?"

"Right. Betty, bless her, offered her resignation, but Cathy talked her out of it. We both suggested Betty take a leave of absence for a month or so. Then, if she was ready, she could come back into the practice."

The waiter appeared with their entrees, which he put down beside their salad plates. They began to eat, although it was apparent from the food left on both plates that they didn't have much appetite. Finally, after turning down the waiter's offer to wrap the remaining food for them, they headed for the front door of the restaurant.

Both pulled their coats tighter as the chill wind hit them outside. Pointing to the sky, Kelly said, "Jack, it's snowing again."

"You know, I haven't been paying any attention to the weather forecast. Or to the calendar, for that matter." He thought for a minute. "Do you know what day this is?"

"It's Monday," Kelly said.

"Not just Monday. It's almost Christmas Eve. And it's snowing." He looked at the flurries coming down around them. "Think we'll have a white Christmas?"

Kelly took Jack's arm as they shuffled through the snow together. "White Christmas or not, I believe we'll have a lot to celebrate this year."

Watch for Dr. Richard Mabry's next novel, coming next summer.

Catherine Hoover (known to her friends as Cat and to her patients as Dr. Hoover) heard the ring of the front doorbell just as she was about to hurry through the kitchen to the garage where her car sat.

She didn't want to take the time to stop and answer the bell. She really hadn't even had time to come home at lunch, but Darren was out of town, and she'd forgotten to let the dog out this morning before she left for the office. If she didn't want to clean up a mess, it was best to hurry home and take care of that chore. She found that shouting, "Go do your business" to her canine companion had little effect, but finally the deed was done.

Cat paused as the ring of the front door chime faded. The local TV news had run a feature just yesterday about packages disappearing from porches. What if... She sighed and reversed direction. It would only take another minute or two for her to open the front door, check to see if FedEx or UPS had left a package, and bring it in if one were there.

Through the pane of glass beside the front door, Cat could see a black panel van just pulling away. It wasn't the familiar dark brown of UPS, nor did it bear the blue and orange logo of FedEx. And it didn't look like a mail delivery truck. Did Amazon have their own delivery service? Whatever it was, she might as well look at what they'd left.

She unlocked the door, took one step onto her front porch, and saw a box about the dimensions of a shoebox lying on the stoop. She reached down to pick it up. The package was wrapped in plain brown paper, with nothing to indicate its origin or contents. *Strange. Maybe it's a mistake.* Cat shook her head.

She tried to think it through logically. *Perhaps this wasn't for me.* Maybe it had been left there by mistake, and the courier would come back for it. Should she simply put the box back on the porch? Then again, she was curious about what was in it. Maybe if she took it into the house and dealt with it later.

Cat wasn't expecting a delivery. Had Darren ordered something without telling her? No, that would be totally out of character for him. If he'd purchased anything, whether a small household appliance or a new car, he would have discussed it with her. And she knew better than to expect a gift from him. Darren wasn't the spontaneous type.

She really needed to get back to the office. But she also was curious about the contents of the package. Her curiosity fought with common sense, and her curiosity won. Before she could change her mind, Cat took the package inside and headed for the kitchen, where she rummaged in the "junk" drawer until she found a pair of scissors with one blade partially broken off. Using the intact half of the instrument, she cut through the tape that held the box closed. When there was no explosion, she let out a breath she didn't know she was holding. Cat dug through the packing peanuts in the box until she found what it contained—a cell phone.

Had Darren arranged for a loaner phone to be sent to their house while his was being repaired? But she'd talked with him just last evening on his cell phone, and it was working then. And wouldn't a loaner or replacement be an iPhone such as they both used? This was nothing like that. Matter of fact, she'd never seen one exactly like this one.

Cat looked at her watch and decided she'd deal with this after she got back home this evening. She was about to put the phone back into the box when it started to vibrate silently. She almost dropped the instrument. Surely this was a mistake—probably a wrong number. She tried to ignore the phone, but that was hard for any physician to do, especially a curious one such as Cat. Finally, when she could stand it no longer, she found the button to answer the call and pushed it.

The voice she heard had a mechanical quality, but the words were clear enough. "Dr. Hoover. This isn't a joke. Carry out my instructions or your husband will die."

She couldn't believe what she was hearing. The phone had been delivered to her house. The voice addressed her by name. This couldn't be a mistake. And so far as she knew, her husband was in Washington, DC, attending a conference. But the voice was threatening his death. How?

It was as though whoever was behind the voice could read her thoughts. "Don't bother calling your husband. No one will answer his cell phone."

"But…"

The voice continued as though Cat hadn't responded. "We'll call you later with more instructions. Keep this phone with you at all times. If you do as we say, perhaps you'll see your husband again."

20190288R00063

Made in the USA
Lexington, KY
03 December 2018